I0611775

HASHKNIFE
of the
DOUBLE BAR 8

HASHKNIFE
of the
DOUBLE BAR 8

By W. C. TUTTLE

FICTION HOUSE PRESS

This story was published in England
under the title, 'Arizona Ways'

ISBN 978-1-64720-097-8

CONTENTS

CHAPTER I

BOOK-KEEPERS

JAMES EATON LEGG hooked his heels over the rounds of his high stool, stretched wearily and looked out through the none-too-clean windows to where a heavy fog almost obscured the traffic. Heavy trucks lumbered past, grinding harshly over the cobbles. Somewhere a street car motorman did a trap-drum effect on his gong ; a ferry boat whistled boomingly. And there was the incessant roar of the everyday noises of the commercial district.

James Eaton Legg was not a prepossessing person. He was less than thirty years of age, slightly beneath medium height, slender. His face was thin, rather boyish, his mild blue eyes hidden behind a pair of glasses. His mouth was wide, and when he yawned wearily he showed a good set of teeth.

For several years James had been a book-keeper with Mellon & Co., Wholesale Grocers, San Francisco —and he was still acting in the same capacity. His slightly stooped shoulders attested to the fact that James had bent diligently over his work. Whether fortunately, or unfortunately, James was an orphan. His mother had died while he was still very young, and when James had just finished high school, his father had gone the way of all flesh.

James was cognisant of the fact that somewhere in the world he had some relatives, but that fact caused him little concern. He remembered that his mother had a sister, who was well endowed with worldly goods, and he also remembered that his father had said that his Aunt Martha would probably die with all her wealth intact.

James turned from his contemplation of the foggy street, and his blue eyes studied the occupants of the big office. There was Henry Marsh, humped like an old buzzard, his long nose close to the ledger page, as he had been the first time James had seen him. He had grown old with Mellon & Co.—so old that he worried about his job.

There were younger men, working adding machines, delving in accounts ; preparing themselves for a life of drudgery. Over in the cashier's cage was David Conley, frozen-faced, pathetic ; as old as Mellon & Co. James shuddered slightly. If he lived to be seventy, and worked faithfully, he might occupy that cage.

James was being paid the munificent sum of seventy dollars a month. He happened to know that David Conley drew one hundred and fifty dollars in his monthly envelope. James shook his head and shifted his gaze back to the window. He did not feel like working. It all seemed so useless ; this idea of putting down figures and adding them up ; eating, sleeping, and coming back to put down more figures.

He turned from contemplation of the wet street, and looked at Blair Mellon, senior member of the firm, who had come in from his private office. He was nearing seventy, thin, stooped, irascible. Nothing seemed to please him. His beady eyes shifted from one employee to another, as he walked slowly. He had made a success of business, but a wreck of himself. The boys of the firm called him "Caucus," because of the fact that once a week he would hold a caucus in the office, at which time he would impress upon them the fact that the firm was everything, and that nothing else mattered.

He would invite suggestions from department heads, and when an idea did not please him he would fly into a rage. James Eaton Legg mildly suggested at one of the caucuses that the firm supply each book-keeper with a fountain pen, in order to economise on lost motions—and nearly lost his job. Not because of trying to increase the efficiency of the book-keeping department, but because fountain pens cost money.

All the firm mail came to Blair Mellon's office, and it was his delight to distribute it. Just now he had several letters which he was passing out. He walked past James, stopped. James was looking at the street again. The old man scowled at the letters in his hand, one of which was addressed to James Eaton Legg. It bore the imprint of a Chicago law firm.

Blair Mellon did not believe that a book-keeper

should waste his time in looking out of the window, but just now he couldn't think of a fitting rebuke ; so he placed the letter on James Legg's desk and went on.

James Legg's mild blue eyes contemplated the name of the law firm on the envelope. It all looked so very legal that James wondered what it might all mean. He drew out the enclosure and read it carefully. Then he removed his glasses, polished them carefully, and read it again. Then he propounded inelegantly, but emphatically,—

" Well, I'll be —— ! "

Blair Mellon had come back past the desk just in time to hear this exclamation. He stopped short and stared at James.

" Mr. Legg ! " he said curtly. " You evidently forget the rule against profanity in this office."

But James Legg ignored everything except his own thoughts.

" If that don't beat everything, what does ? " he queried.

Blair Mellon stared aghast. This was downright mutiny. He struggled for the proper words with which to rebuke this young man.

" Say, Caucus," said James, giving Mellon the nickname he had never heard before, " where do they raise cattle ? "

" Were you speaking to me, sir ? " demanded Mellon.

James realised what he had said, and for a moment his face flushed.

" I beg your pardon, Mr. Mellon."

" I should think you would, sir. Such language ! "

It seemed that all work had ceased in the office. Not even a telephone bell rang.

" Have you any excuse for speaking in such a manner ? " demanded the old man, conscious that every one had heard.

James Eaton Legg surveyed the room. Every eye was upon him. He noticed that even the stenographers had ceased chewing their gum. Then James Legg laughed, as he drew off his black sateen oversleeves and cast them aside. He slid off his stool, almost into the irate Mellon.

" Well, sir ! " the old man's voice creaked.

" Aw, save it for somebody that's working for you," said James Legg easily. " I've quit."

" Quit ? "

" Yes. Strange, isn't it ? " James Legg smiled at the old man. " Book-keepers don't usually quit, do they ? No, they stick to the job until their chin hits their knees, and the undertaker has to put them in a press for two days before they'll fit a casket. I suppose the cashier will pay me off, Mr. Mellon."

" Well—er—yes, sir ! It is just as well that you do quit. This is very, very unusual for an employee of Mellon and Company to——"

" To quit ? " smiled James. " Sets a precedent."

" Ordinarily, we would offer a letter of recommendation, but in a case of——"

" Couldn't use it, but thank you just the same, Mr. Mellon. I am through keeping books. I'm going to take a job where I can breathe fresh air, smoke a cigarette on the job, and swear when **I** please.''

The old man's lean jaw set tightly for a moment, but he said icily :—

" And what are you going to do, if I may ask ? "

" Me ? " James Legg smiled broadly around the room. " I'm going to be a cowpuncher.''

" A—a—what ? "

" A cowboy, if that makes it plain to you.''

One of the stenographers tittered. She had her own idea of a cowboy, possibly not from the real article ; so she might be forgiven for seeing humour in Legg's statement. He flushed a little, turned on his heels and went to the wash-room, every one looking after him. Blair Mellon broke the spell with :—

" The incident is over, I believe, ladies and gentlemen.''

Which was sufficient to put them all back to work, while James Eaton Legg accepted his pay from the stiff-faced cashier and walked out into the foggy street. He felt just a little weak over it all. It was hard to realise that he was at last without a job.

It was the first time in years that he had been without a job, and the situation rather appalled him, and he stopped on a corner, wondering whether he hadn't been just a trifle abrupt in quitting Mellon & Company.

But he realised that the die was cast ; so he went to his boarding-house and to his room, where he secured an old atlas. Spreading out a map **on** the bed, he studied the Western States. Arizona seemed to appeal to him ; so he ran a pencil-point along the railroad lines, wondering just where in Arizona he would care to make his start.

The pencil-point stopped at Blue Wells, and he instinctively made a circle around the name. It seemed rather isolated, and James Legg had an idea that it must be a cattle country. Something or somebody was making a noise at his door ; so he got up from the bed.

He opened the door and found that the noise had been made by a dog ; a rough-coated mongrel, yellowish-red, with one black eye, which gave him a devil-may-care expression. He was dirty and wet, panting from a hard run, but he sat up and squinted at James Legg, his tongue hanging out.

" Where did you come from, dog ? " demanded James. " I don't think I have ever seen you before."

The dog held up one wet paw, and James shook hands with him solemnly. Came the sound of a heavy voice downstairs, and the dog shot past James and went under the bed. The voice was audible now, and James could distinguish the high-pitched voice of the landlady raised in protest.

" But I tell ye I seen him come in here, ma'am," declared the heavy voice. " A kind of a yaller one, he was."

" But no one in this house owns a dog," protested the landlady. " We don't allow dogs in here."

" Don't ye ? And have ye the rules printed in

dog language, so that the dogs would know it, ma'am ? Belike he's in one of the halls, tryin' to hide."

"I'm sure you're mistaken, officer. But I'll go with you, if you care to make a search of the halls."

"I'll do that, ma'am."

James closed his door, leaving only a crack wide enough for him to see the landlady, followed by a big burly policeman, come to the head of the stairs. They came past his door, and he heard them farther down the hall. The dog was still under the bed, and as they came back James stepped into the hall.

"We are looking for a yellow dog, Mr. Legg," explained the landlady. "You haven't seen one, have you ? "

"Sort of yaller and red," supplemented the officer.

James shook his head. "Must be an important yellow dog to have the police hunting for him."

"He's important to me," growled the officer. "Jist a dirty stray, so he is."

"But why are you hunting for a stray dog, officer ? "

"Because he's a dangerous dog. I threw a rock at him, tryin' to chase him off me beat, and the dirty cur picked up the rock and brought it back to me."

"A retriever, eh ? "

"I dunno his breed."

"But that doesn't make him dangerous."

" Then I took a kick at him and he bit me, so he did. He tore the leg of me pants and I had to go home and change. I didn't no more than get back on me beat, when there he was, probably lookin' for another chance at me legs. But I took after him and I was sure he ran in here."

" Well, I'm sure he never did," said the landlady. " But we'll look in the other halls."

James went back in the room and found the dog sitting in the middle of the floor, one ear cocked up, his brown eyes fixed on James, his tongue hanging out, as if he had heard all of the conversation and was laughing at the policeman.

James held out his hand, and they shook seriously.

" Dog," said James seriously, " you did what I've often thought I'd like to do—bite a policeman. I swore out loud in Mellon and Company's office, and you bit a cop. We're a disgraceful pair. I'm wondering if you're a cattle dog "—James sighed heavily—" Well, anyway, you're as much of a cattle dog as I am a cowpuncher. Sit down and make yourself at home."

It was half an hour later that James Eaton Legg walked out of his room, carrying a heavy valise, while behind him came the dog, walking carefully, peering around the legs of his newly-found master.

At the foot of the stairs they met the landlady. She stared at the dog and at James.

" That was the dog the policeman was looking for ! " she exclaimed in a horrified screech. " Don't let him come toward me! You get that dog out of here, Mr. Legg! You know we don't allow dogs in here. Take him——"

"That dog," said James calmly, "is very particular who he bites, ma'am. If my bill is ready——"

"Oh, are you leaving us, Mr. Legg?"

"Yes'm, me and—er—Geronimo are leaving. If any mail comes for me, forward it to Jim Legg, Blue Wells, Arizona."

"Oh, yes. Blue Wells, Arizona. Are you going out there for your health?"

"Well," said Jim Legg, as he paid his bill, "I don't know just how it'll affect me physically. It'll probably be a good thing for Geronimo—give him a change of diet, and for the good of the police force I suppose I better phone for a taxi."

And thus did Jim Legg, erstwhile James Eaton Legg, quit his job, adopt a dog, and start for Blue Wells, just an isolated spot on the map of Arizona —all in the same day.

CHAPTER II

IT was the biggest two-handed poker game ever played in Blue Wells, and when "Antelope Jim" Neal, owner of the Blue Wells Oasis Saloon, raked in the last pot, "Tex" Alden rubbed the back of his hand across his dry lips and shut his weary eyes. He had lost eight thousand dollars.

"Is that all, Tex?" asked Neal, and his voice held a hope that the big cowboy would answer in the affirmative. The game had never ceased for thirty-six hours.

"As far as I'm concerned," said Tex slowly. "I don't owe yuh anythin', do I?"

"Not a cent, Tex. Have a drink?"

"Yeah—whisky."

Tex got to his feet, stretching himself wearily. He was well over six feet tall, habitually gloomy of countenance. His hair was black, as were his jowls, even after a close shave. There were dark circles around his brown eyes, and his hand trembled as he poured out a full glass of liquor and swallowed it at a gulp.

"Here's better luck next time, Tex," said Neal.

"Throw it into yuh," said Tex shortly. "But as far as luck is concerned——"

" It did kinda break against yuh, Tex."

" Kinda l Well, see yuh later."

Tex adjusted his hat and walked outside, while Neal went to his room at the back of the saloon, threw off his clothes, and piled into bed. At the bar several cowboys added another drink to their already large collection, and marvelled at the size of Tex Alden's losses.

" 'F I lost that much, I'd have a good time buyin' any Christmas presents for m' friends, next December," said Johnny Grant, a diminutive cowboy from the AK ranch.

" There ain't that much money," declared " Eskimo " Swensen, two hundred pounds of authority on any subject, who also drew forty dollars per month from the AK. " It takes over sixteen years of steady work, without spendin' a cent, to make that much money. Never let anybody tell yuh that there is any eight thousand in one lump sum."

" And that statement carries my endorsement," nodded the third hired man of the AK, " Oyster " Shell, a wry-necked, buck-toothed specimen of the genus cowboy, whose boot-heels were so badly run over on the outer sides that it was difficult for him to attain his full height.

" There has been that much," argued Johnny. " I 'member one time when I had——"

" Eighty," interrupted Oyster. " Yuh got so drunk you seen a coupla extra ciphers, Johnny. I feel m'self stretchin' a point to let yuh have eighty."

" I votes for eight," declared Eskimo heavily.

" Eight thousand ain't so awful much," said " Doc " Painter, the bartender, who wore a curl on his forehead, and who was a human incense stick, reeking of violets.

Johnny looked closely at Dock, placed his Stetson on the bar and announced :—

" Mister Rockerbilt will now take the stand and speak on ' Money I Have Seen.' "

" Misser Rockerbilt," Oyster bowed his head against the bar and stepped on his new hat before he could recover it.

" A-a-a-aw, —— ! " snorted the bartender. " I've seen more than eight thousand, I'll tell yuh that. I've had——"

" Now, Doc," warned Eskimo. " Seein' and havin' are two different things. We all know that yuh came from a wealthy family, who gave yuh everythin' yuh wanted, and nothin' yuh needed. But if you ever try to make us believe that you had eight thousand dollars, we'll sure kick yuh out of our Sunday school, because yuh never came by it honestly."

" Yeah, and yuh don't need to say we ain't got no Sunday school," added Oyster hastily. " Last Sunday——"

" I heard about it."

The bartender carefully polished a glass, breathing delicately upon it the while.

" Lemme have that glass a minute," said Johnny, and the unsuspecting bartender gave it to him. Johnny selected a place on the bar-rail and proceeded to smash the glass.

" What the —— did yuh do that for ? " demanded the bartender hotly.

" What for ? " Johnny lifted his brows and stared at the bartender with innocent eyes.

" Yea-a-ah ! Why smash that glass ? "

" Well, yuh can't expect anybody to ever drink out of it, could yuh ? After you yawnin' upon it thataway, Doc. I know—well I don't want to draw it.'

" That don't hurt the glass ! "

" Well, of all things ! " shrilled Oyster. " As long as the glass don't get hurt, everythin' is all right. I'll betcha he's yawned upon every glass he's got. If we was ever goin' to drink in this place again, I'd argue in favour of smashin' every glass he's got on that back bar."

And the bartender knew that the AK outfit were entirely capable of doing just such a thing. But they were not quite drunk enough to accept Oyster's suggestion. At any rate their minds were diverted by the entrance of " Scotty " Olson, the big lumbering sheriff of Blue Wells, whose sense of humour was not quite as big nor as lively as a fever germ.

Scotty wore a buffalo-horn moustache, which matched the huge eyebrows that shaded his little eyes. He was a powerful person, huge of hand, heavy-voiced ; rather favouring a sawed-off, double-barrelled shotgun, which he handled with one hand.

" The law is among us," said Johnny seriously. " Have a little drink, Mister Law ? "

"No." Scotty was without finesse.

"Have a cigar?" asked Eskimo.

"No."

"Have a chaw?" queried Oyster pleasantly.

"No. I was just talkin' with the preacher."

"Tryin' to reform yuh?" asked Johnny.

"Reform? No. He wants to know which one of you punchers tin-canned his horse?"

The three cowboys looked at each other. Their expression of amazement was rather overdone. The bartender chuckled, and Johnny turned quickly.

"What is so funny about it, Doc?" he demanded. "It's no laughin' matter, I'd tell a man," he turned to the sheriff.

"You surely don't think we'd do a thing like that, Sheriff."

"I dunno." The sheriff scratched his head, tilting his hat down over one eye.

"My! That would be sacrilege!" exclaimed Eskimo.

"The Last Warnin'," corrected Oyster seriously, not knowing the meaning of sacrilege. The Last Warnin' was an ancient sway-backed white horse, which the minister drove to an old wobble-wheeled buggy. He had a mean eye and a propensity for digging his old hammer-shaped head into the restaurant garbage cans.

"It ain't funny," said the sheriff. "There ain't nothin' funny about tin-cannin' a horse. Louie Sing's big copper slop-can is missin', and Louie swears that he's goin' to sue the preacher. I reckon it's up to you boys to pay the preacher for his horse and Louie Sing for his copper can. The preacher says that fifty is about right for the horse, and Louie swears that he can't replace the can for less than ten."

"Well," sighed Johnny, "all I can say is that you and the preacher and the Chink are plumb loco, if you think we're goin' to pay sixty dollars for a—for somethin' we never done."

"Where'd we get sixty dollars—even if we was guilty?" wondered Oyster.

"Yuh might make it in Sunday school," suggested the bartender.

"In Sunday school? What do yuh mean?"

"Well," grinned Doc, "I hear that one of yuh put a four-bit piece in the collection plate and took out ninety-five cents in change."

Whether or not there was any truth in the statement, Johnny Grant took sudden exceptions to it and flung himself across the bar, pawing at the bartender, whose shoulders collided with the stacked glassware on the back bar, as he tried to escape the clawing hands.

"Stop that!" yelled the sheriff.

He rushed at Johnny, trying to save the worthy bartender from assault, but one of his big boots became entangled with the feet of Oyster Shell, and he sprawled on his face, narrowly missing the bar-rail, while into him fell Eskimo Olson, backward, of course, his spurs catching in the sheriff's vest and shirt and almost disrobing him.

With a roar of wrath the sheriff got to his feet, made an ineffectual swing at Eskimo, and ran at

Oyster, who had backed to the centre of the room, holding a chair in both hands. The sheriff was so wrathy that he ignored the chair, until Oyster flung it down against his shins, and the sheriff turned a complete somersault, which knocked all the breath out of him.

Johnny Grant had swung around on the bar in time to see the sheriff crash down, ignoring the perspiring bartender, who, armed with a bottle, had backed to the end of the bar. The sheriff got to his feet, one foot still fast between the rounds of the chair, and looked vacantly around. Then he grinned foolishly and headed for the front door, dragging the chair.

It tripped him as he went across the threshold, and he fell on his knees outside. Then he got to his feet, tore the offending chair loose, flung it viciously out into the street, and went lurching toward his office, scratching his head, as if wondering what it was all about.

" Knocked back seven generations," whooped Eskimo, as he clung to Johnny Grant, who in turn was hugging Oyster.

" Mamma Mine, I hope t' die ! " whooped Johnny. " Oh, don't show me no more ! Ha, ha, ha, ha, ha ! He never even seen that chair ! "

They went into more paroxysms of mirth, while the bartender smoothed his vest, placed his bottle back behind the bar, and got a broom to sweep up the broken glassware. He knew that he was forgotten for a while at least.

CHAPTER III

TEX ALDEN had left the Oasis and sauntered
down the street to where a weathered sign pro-
claimed the office of Lee Barnhardt, Attorney-at-
Law. Barnhardt was a lean, hatchet-faced, keen-
eyed sort of person, possibly forty-five years of
age, whose eyes were rather too close together, ears
small and clinging close to his bony head, and
chin was wedge-shaped. His neck was so long
and thin that it was the general opinion in Blue
Wells that on Sunday Barnhardt wore a cuff
around his neck instead of a collar.

Tex Alden and Lee Barnhardt had considerable
in common, as Tex was manager of the X Bar 6
cattle outfit, while Barnhardt was legal counsel
and manager for the same outfit. Tex had always
borne a fairly good reputation, except that he was
an inveterate gambler. People admitted that
Barnhardt was shrewd, even if they did not like
him.

Barnhardt was busily engaged in cleaning out
his old cob pipe when Tex walked in and sat down,
and like all lawyers he kept Tex waiting until the
pipe was cleaned, filled and lighted. Then he

turned around on his creaking swivel-chair and fixed his cold eyes upon Tex.

" Well ? " he managed to say, between puffs.

" Well ! " snorted Tex. " I just finished losing the eight thousand dollars I got for that shipment to 'Frisco."

Barnhardt's eyebrows lifted slightly and he sucked heavily on his extinguished pipe, staring steadily at Tex. Then :—

" You lost it all, eh ? Playing poker with Neal ? "

Tex nodded wearily. Barnhardt leaned back in his old chair, squinting narrowly at the ceiling.

" That's a lot of money, Tex," he said thoughtfully. " It puts you in pretty bad, don't yuh think ? "

" Sure. That's why I came over here, Lee."

" Is that so ? Thinking, of course, that I can square it for yuh," Barnhardt laughed wryly. " It's quite a job to explain away eight thousand dollars, Tex. I don't know why you didn't bring that cheque to me."

" They made it out in my name," said Tex, as if that might mitigate the fact that he had used eight thousand belonging to the X Bar 6 outfit.

" That didn't cause it to belong to you," reminded Barnhardt. " They can jail yuh for that, Tex. It's plain embezzlement. I've got to account for that eight thousand dollars."

" How soon, Lee ? "

The lawyer frowned thoughtfully. He knew he could defer the accounting for a long time, but what good would that do Tex Alden, whose monthly salary was seventy-five dollars.

"Got something in sight, Tex?" he asked.

"Not yet," Tex studied the toes of his dusty boots. "But yuh never can tell what might turn up."

"I see."

Barnhardt relaxed and lighted his pipe. After a few puffs he said :—

"I think the Santa Rita pay-roll comes in to-night."

"Thasso?" Tex stared at Barnhardt. "How do yuh know?"

"Chet Le Moyne rode in a while ago. He always shows up just ahead of the pay-roll and takes it back to the Santa Rita himself."

Chet Le Moyne was paymaster of the Santa Rita Mine, which employed close to three hundred men. The mine was located about twelve miles from Blue Wells. Le Moyne was a handsome sort of a person, dark-haired, dark-eyed, athletic although slender. Like Tex Alden, he was an inveterate gambler, although not inclined to plunge wildly.

"I think probably he went out to the Taylor ranch," offered Barnhardt casually. "He never does stay very long in town."

Tex scowled at his boots, and tried to make himself believe that it didn't make any difference to him if Le Moyne went out to see Marion Taylor. But down in his heart he knew it did—a lot of difference. Paul Taylor owned a small ranch about two miles south of Blue Wells, and there was no one to deny that Marion Taylor was the best-looking girl in that country.

Even Lee Barnhardt had cast covetous eyes in that direction, but Marion showed small favour to the thin-faced lawyer. In fact, she had showed little favour to any of the men, treating them all alike. Perhaps Tex and Le Moyne had been the most persistent suitors.

Old Paul Taylor, often known as " The Apostle," did not favour any certain one as a son-in-law. They were all welcome to call, as far as he was concerned. Between himself, his son, a wild-riding, hot-headed youth, known as " Buck," and one cowboy, a half-breed Navajo, known as " Peeler," they managed to eke out a living. Buck and Peeler were as wild as the ranges around Blue Wells, and The Apostle was not far behind, when it came to making the welkin ring. The Apostle was a typical old-time cattleman, who hated to see civilisation crowding into the ranges.

Barnhardt studied Tex, while the big cowboy humped in a chair and studied the floor. Finally Tex lifted his head and looked at Barnhardt.

" Just why did yuh tell me about the Santa Rita pay-roll comin' in to-night, Lee ? "

" No reason, Tex ; just conversation, I reckon. It must run close to thirty thousand dollars. Le Moyne had one man with him. That train gets in about nine o'clock. Le Moyne probably will ride straight for the mine. That's quite a lump of money, Tex. I hear they always pay off in gold, because there's quite a lot of Mexicans working there, and they like the yellow money."

" Uh-huh." Tex's eyes narrowed as he looked at Barnhardt. " Thirty thousand is a lot of money."

" It sure **is** plenty," nodded Barnhardt. " More than a man could make in a lifetime out here."

Tex got to his feet and rolled a cigarette.

" Yuh can keep that eight thousand under **cover** a while, can'tcha, Lee ? "

" For a while, Tex—sure thing."

" Thank yuh, Lee. *Adios.*"

Tex sauntered out and the lawyer looked after him, a crooked smile on his lips, feeling that he and Tex Alden understood each other perfectly. He could look from his window and see Tex get his horse at the livery-stable and ride away.

The sheriff did not go back to the Oasis Saloon that afternoon. The whole incident wasn't quite clear in his mind. He had a lump on his forehead, where he hit the floor, and one shin was skinned from the chair, but he wasn't quite sure just who was to blame for it all. Anyway, he wasn't sure that they had tin-canned the minister's horse with Louie Sing's copper can.

He wished Al Porter, his deputy, were there. Al knew how to get along with those fellows from the AK. But Al had gone to Encinas that afternoon to see his girl, and wouldn't be back until late that night, even if he were fortunate enough to catch a freight train. Encinas was twelve miles east of Blue Wells.

The election of Scotty Olson had been more **or**

less of a joke. There had been quite a lot of mud-slinging between the Republican and Democrat candidates, and a bunch of the boys got together and induced Scotty to run independently. And while the two favourites in the race, to use a racing parlance, tried to cut each other down in the stretch, Scotty, hardly knowing what it was all about, won the election.

He had appointed Al Porter, a former deputy sheriff, to act as his deputy and mentor, and the office was really run by Al, much to the amusement of every one concerned, except Scotty, who was satisfied that he was making a big reputation for himself.

Oyster Shell, Johnny Grant, and Eskimo Swensen continued to make merry at the Oasis, mostly at the expense of the bartender, who writhed under punishment but grinned in spite of it, because he owned an interest in the Oasis, with Neal, and the boys of the AK were good patrons.

It was after dark when Johnny Grant decided that it was time to go back to the ranch. He announced the fact, and his two companions suddenly found themselves of the same notion.

Out to the hitch-rack they weaved their erratic way, only to find the rack empty of horses. Johnny leaned against the end-post and rubbed his nose, while Oyster walked up and down both sides of the rack, running one hand along the top bar.

" Nossin' here," he declared. " 'F there's a horsh at thish rack, I can't fin' him. Whatcha shay, Eskimo ? "

" I shed," replied Eskimo heavily, " I shed, tha's queer."

" Isn' it queer ? " asked Oyster. " I ask you open and 'bove board, ain't it queer ? Whazza-matter, Johnny—gone in a tranch ? "

" He's drunk," declared Eskimo, trying to slap the top bar of the rack with his hand, and hitting his chin instead.

" And yo're cold shober," said Oyster. " Losin' a horsh makes you so mad that you bite the hitch-rack. Go ahead and gnaw it f'r me, Eskimo. Johnny, whatcha think, eh ? "

" I think," said Johnny thickly, " I think it's between the sheriff and the preacher. Shomebody took our horshes."

" He's commencin' to wake up, Eskimo," said Oyster. " He's had a vision, that's what he's had. Oh my, tha' boy is clever. Let's have a vote on which one we kill firsht—sheriff or preacher."

" I vote for the sheriff," declared Eskimo. " We need lossa gospel 'round here. Let's kill the sheriff firsht. Then when the preacher preaches the funeral shervice, if he shays a good word for Scotty Olson, we'll kill the preacher and let the morals of thish here country go plumb to —— "

" Let's not kill anybody—yet," advised Johnny. " Lissen t' me, will yuh. Didja ever hear that sayin' about whom the gods would destroy, they firsht make awful mad ? Didja ? Well, let's make Scotty Olson awful mad, eh ? "

" But we ain't gods," reminded Oyster.

" Tha's a fact," admitted Johnny. " We ain't

gods. But," hopefully, "mebbe we'll do until shome better ones comes along."

"We're jist as good," declared Eskimo. "I'm jist as good as any I've ever sheen—prob'ly a lot better. Let's go ahead and do shomethin'. Whazza programme, Johnny?"

"First," said Johnny, "we'll ask Scotty in a ladylike manner what he done with our horshes. And I don't want you pelicans to forget that you're as drunk as a pair of boiled owls. C'mon."

They weaved across the street. Johnny Grant lost his hat, and after several minutes' search, it was discovered that Eskimo was standing on it.

"Thirty dollars gone t' ——!" wailed Johnny.

"Aw, it ain't hurt!" snorted Eskimo. "Jist dirty, thasall."

"After you wearin' it on one of yore big feet all over the street? I can see the moon through it."

"Wonnerful!" gasped Oyster. "I tell yuh the boy's got shecond shight. Ha, ha, ha, ha, ha! There ain't no moon."

They managed to reach the door of the sheriff's office. A light from the front window attested to the fact that Scotty Olson was in the office, and he answered their knock.

"What do you want?" he asked. Johnny leaned against the door-sill, his torn and dusty sombrero pulled rakishly over one eye.

"We want you to shettle a question that's been botherin' us, Scotty. C'n we come in?"

"All right," said Scotty grudgingly.

He stepped aside and the three cowboys came in.

They had been in the office many times, but not in this same mood.

"My, my, thish is a nice office!" exclaimed Eskimo. "Gotta desk and a chair and a lot of outlaw's pitchers on the walls!"

"What question did you want answered?" asked Scotty nervously. He suspected them of having ulterior reasons.

"The question is thish," said Johnny. "What did you do with our horshes?"

"A roan, a bay, and a sorrel," enumerated Oyster. The sheriff shook his head.

"I ain't seen yore horses."

"Jist try and remember," urged Johnny. "Try and recall the fact that you got mad at us and took 'em away."

"Aw-w-w!" snorted Scotty vacantly. "I can't remember nothin' of the kind."

"I'll betcha," said Oyster seriously, "I'll betcha he's got 'em in one of his cells."

"Aw-w-w-w!" Scotty goggled at him. "That's a thing to say. Put a horse in a cell!"

"Mind if we look?" queried Johnny.

"Well, of all the drunken ideas! No, I don't care if yuh look. Yuh can't put a horse in a cell!"

He turned on his heel and led them to the rear of the building, where a series of three cells had been built in, leaving a corridor down the centre. The doors were heavily barred and fitted with spring locks. Just now there were no occupants in the Blue Wells jail, and the doors sagged partly open.

Scotty, half-angry, more than half disgusted, swung the door of the first cell wide open and stepped partly inside, turning to let the cowboys see for themselves that there were no horses in the cell, when Eskimo seemed to stumble, flung his weight against the door, which promptly snapped shut, locking the sheriff in his own cell.

" Hey ! You —— fool ! " yelled Scotty. " Whatcha tryin' to do, anyway ? "

" Look what you done ! " wailed Johnny. " You've locked the sheriff in his own jail. Now, you've done it. My, my ! "

" Go and get the keys out of my desk," ordered the sheriff. " They're in the top drawer."

The three cowboys trooped obediently out through the office, extinguished the lamp, closed the door, and stood on the edge of the sidewalk, chuckling with unholy glee.

" Let's see if he put our broncs in his stable," suggested Johnny. But the sheriff's stable was empty. They went to the livery-stable and found it locked.

" How about visitin' the preacher ? " asked Eskimo.

" He never done it," declared Oyster. " That jigger is too timid to go near a bronc. I'll betcha that smart sheriff jist turned 'em loose on us, that's what he done. We might as well git a room at the hotel, or walk back to the ranch."

" I'll walk," said Eskimo. " I stayed one night at that old hotel and the bedbugs et holes in my boots."

" Shall we let the sheriff loose before we go ? "
asked Oyster.

" Let 'm alone," said Johnny. " Somebody will
turn him loose after a while, and I don't want to be
here when they do. Eskimo, if I was you, I'd buy
a bottle to take along with us. It's a long, hard
walk."

" That's a pious notion," declared Eskimo, and
they went weaving back toward the Oasis.

CHAPTER IV

JIMMY GETS HIS DANDER UP

JIM LEGG sprawled on a seat in the day-coach and tried to puzzle out from a time-table just when they would arrive at Blue Wells. It was a mixed train, both passenger and freight, stopping at every station along the branch line; sixty miles of starts and stops, and the highest speed would not exceed twenty miles per hour.

It had been sweltering hot, and Jim Legg's once-white collar had melted to the consistency of a dish-rag. But the shades of night had brought a cool breeze, and the gruff brakeman had assured him that the train would probably arrive on time.

Not that it made much difference to Jim Legg. He had never seen Blue Wells. To him it was merely a name. He had been forced to leave Geronimo to the tender mercies of a hard-faced express messenger, and had seen him tied to a trunk-handle in the express car.

It suddenly occurred to Jim Legg that he had made no provisions for feed and water for the dog. It did not occur to him that the messenger might be human enough to do this for the dog. The engine was whistling a station call, and Jim Legg resolved to investigate for himself.

The train clanked to a stop at the little station, and Jim Legg dropped off the steps, making his way up to the baggage car, where the messenger and a brakeman were unloading several packages. Jim noticed that the weather-beaten sign on the front of the depot showed it to be Encinas, the town where the deputy sheriff's sweetheart lived.

The brakeman went on toward the engine, and Jim Legg got into the express car. Geronimo's tie-rope had been shifted to a trunk farther up the aisle, and the messenger stood just beyond him, looking over a sheaf of way-bills by the dim light of a lantern.

The train jerked ahead, but Jim Legg did not notice that they were travelling again, until the train had gained considerable speed. The messenger turned and came back toward the door, not noticing in the dim light that he had a new passenger. The dog reared up and put his paws on the messenger's overall-clad leg.

But only for a moment. The messenger whirled around and kicked the dog back against the trunk.

" Keep off me, —— yuh ! " he rasped.

The dog rolled over, but came to his feet, fangs bared.

" Try to bite me, yill yuh ? " snarled the messenger.

He glanced around for some sort of a weapon, evidently not caring to get within kicking distance of the dog again, when Jim Legg spoke mildly :—

" You really shouldn't do that."

The messenger whirled around and stared at Jim

Legg. He did not recognise him as the man who had put the dog in the car at the main line.

" What are you doin' in my car ? " he demanded.

Jim Legg shifted uneasily.

" Well, I—I'm watching you mistreat a dumb brute, it seems. Tha's my dog, and I didn't put him on here to be kicked."

" Your dog, eh ? "

The messenger came closer. He recognised Jim now.

" Got on at Encinas, eh ? "

" I think that was the name. The train started, and I had no chance to get back to the coach, you see."

" Yeah, I see. But that don't make any difference to me. Nobody is allowed to ride in here. You'll have to get off at Blue Wells."

" Is that the next station ? "

" Yeah. We'll be there in a few minutes." He looked back at the dog. " You hadn't ought to ship a dog like that. He's no earthly good, and he tried to bite me just now."

" You're a liar ! "

It was the first time Jim Legg had ever said that to any one, and this time he had said it without a thought of the consequences. It seemed the natural thing to say.

" I'm a liar, eh ? "

The messenger would weigh close on two hundred pounds and was as hard as nails.

" Yes, sir," declared Jim Legg. " If you say that Geronimo tried to bite you just now, you're a liar. I could report you for kicking that dog."

"Oh, you could, could yuh? The company ain't responsible for dogs. You never checked him. He's just ridin' here because I was good enough to take him in; just a dead-head."

"Good enough, eh?"

Jim Legg took off his glasses, put them in a case, and tucked them in his pocket. The messenger came closer. The train was whistling, and they felt the slight jerk as the brakes were applied.

"I saw you kick that dog," said Jim calmly, although his heart was hammering against his ribs. "No man would do a thing like that. It was a dirty trick—and then you try to lie out of it."

"Why, you little four-eyed pup!" snorted the messenger. "I'll make you take that back. Anyway, you've got no right in this car, and I'm justified in throwin' yuh off."

Jim Legg threw out his hands in protest to any such an action. He had never fought anybody, knew nothing of self-defence. But the messenger evidently mistook Jim's attitude, and swung a right-hand smash at his head. And Jim's clumsy attempt to duck the blow caused the messenger to crash his knuckles against the top of Jim's head. The impact of the fist sent Jim reeling back against a pile of trunks, dazed, bewildered, while the messenger, his right hand all but useless, swore vitriolically and headed for Jim again.

But the force of the blow had stirred something in the small man's brain; the fighting instinct, perhaps. And in another moment they were locked together in the centre of the car. The train was lurching to a stop, but they did not know it.

The messenger's arms were locked around Jim's body, while Jim's legs were wrapped around those of the messenger, which caused them to fall heavily, struggling, making queer sounds, while Geronimo, reared the full length of his rope, made an unearthly din of barks, whines, and growls, as he fought to get into the mêlée.

The train yanked ahead, going faster this time. Jim managed to get his right hand free and to get his fingers around the messenger's ear, trying ineffectually to bounce the messenger's head on the hard floor.

His efforts, while hardly successful, caused the messenger to roll over on top of Jim, who clung to the ear and managed to roll on top again. They were getting perilously near the wide door. Suddenly the messenger loosened one hand and began a series of short body punches against Jim's ribs, causing him to relax his hold on the ear. It also forced Jim to slacken his scissor hold on the messenger's legs.

Quickly the messenger doubled up his legs, forcing his knees into Jim's middle, hurling him over and sidewise. But the shift had given Jim a chance to get both arms around the messenger's neck, and when Jim swung over and felt himself dropping into space, he took the messenger right along with him.

They landed with a crash on the edge of a cut,
rolled slowly through a patch of brush, and came to
rest at the bottom of the cut. Fortunately Jim
was uppermost at the finish. The breath had all
been knocked from his body, and he was bruised
from heels to hair.

He separated himself from his former antagonist,
and pumped some air into his aching lungs. The
train was gone. Jim looked up at the star-specked
Arizona sky and wondered what it was all about.
It suddenly struck him funny, and he laughed, a
queer little creaky laugh. It sounded like a few
notes from a wheezy old accordion he had heard a
blind man playing in San Francisco. San Francisco
and the Mellon Company seemed a long way off
just now.

He crawled to the track level. There was no
sign of the train. Everything was very still, except
the dull hum of the telegraph wires along the
right-of-way fence. Then the messenger began
swearing, wondering aloud what was the matter.
Jim Legg got to his feet and filled his lungs with
the good desert air. He looked back toward the
cut where he had left his opponent.

" Shut up ! " he yelled. " You got whipped, and
that's all there is to it."

And then Jim Legg guessed which was Blue
Wells, and started limping along the track. The
stopping and starting of the train between stations
meant nothing to Jim Legg. He did not suspect that
the first stop had been because a red lantern had
been placed in the middle of the track near the

Broken Cañon trestle, thereby stopping the train, and that just now three masked men were smashing through the safe, which contained the Santa Rita pay-roll. There, three men had cut the express car, forced the engineer to drive his engine to within about two miles of Blue Wells, where they stopped him, and escorted both engineer and fireman back to the express car.

The absence of the messenger bothered them, because they were afraid he had suspected a hold-up and had run away, looking for help. At any rate, they went about their business in a workmanlike manner, and a few minutes after the stop they had exploded enough dynamite to force the safe to give up its golden treasure.

Quickly they removed the two canvas sacks. One of the men stepped to the doorway. Somewhere a voice was singing. The road from Blue Wells to the AK ranch paralleled the railroad at this point.

" Come on," said the man at the door.

Swiftly they dropped out of the car, leaving the engineer and fireman alone. A lantern on a trunk illuminated the car. Suddenly the engineer ran across the car and picked up the messenger's sawed-off Winchester shotgun, which had fallen behind a trunk during the fight between the messenger and Jim Legg.

He pumped in a cartridge and sprang to the door. Just out beyond the right-of-way fence he could see three shadowy figures, which were moving. Then he threw up the shotgun and the express car fairly jarred from the report of the heavy buck-shot load.

The distance was great enough to give the charge of buckshot a chance to spread to a maximum degree, and none of the leaden pellets struck the mark. But just the same the three shadowy figures became prone objects.

Again came the long spurt of orange flame from the door of the express car, and more buckshot whined through the weeds.

" What kinda whisky was that yuh bought ? " queried the voice of Johnny Grant from among the weeds.

" Well, if you think I'm goin' t' let any train crew heave buckshot at me, yo're crazy," declared Eskimo Swensen, and proceeded to shoot at the glow from the express car door.

" H'rah f'r us ! " whooped Oyster, and unlimbered two shots from his six-shooter. His aim was a bit uncertain and it is doubtful if either bullet even hit the car.

Wham ! Skee-e-e-e-e ! Another handful of buck-shot mowed the grass. Three six-shooters blazed back at the flash of the shotgun, and their owners shifted locations as fast as possible, because those last buckshot came too close for comfort.

Then came a lull. In fact the shooting ceased entirely. The three men in the grass saw the light go out in the car. There was no noise, except the panting of the engine, its headlight cutting a pathway of silver across the Arizona hills. Minute after minute passed. It was too dark to see an object against the car or engine, and the three men in the grass did not see the engineer and fireman crawl along to the engine and sneak into the cab.

" Where's that —— murderer with the riot-gun ? " queried Eskimo Swensen. He was anxious to continue the battle.

" Sh-h-h-h-h ! " cautioned Johnny. " Somebody comin'."

They could see the vague bulk of a man coming along the track. Then it passed the end of the express car, blending in with it. The three cowboys could hear the crunch of gravel, as the newcomer walked along the car, and they heard him climb inside. Came the tiny glow of a match, the snappy bark of a dog. A few moments later came the thud of two bodies hitting the gravel.

" I whipped him, Geronimo," they heard a voice say.

" I thought Geronimo was dead or in jail," snorted Eskimo.

Then the engine awoke and the part of a train started backing down the track, but there was no more shooting. Once away from that immediate spot the engineer put on more power, and went roaring back toward where they had cut loose from the rest of the train.

The three cowboys sat up in the grass and watched the dim figures of a man and a dog, heading toward Blue Wells, while from far down the rail-road came the shrill whistle of the locomotive.

Johnny Grant got to his feet, and was joined

by Eskimo and Oyster. The shooting had sobered them considerably, and when Eskimo produced the bottle, Johnny shoved it aside.

" Aw, to —— with the stuff ! " he said. " I've been seein' too many things already. Let's go home before we get killed for bein' on earth."

" I dunno," said Eskimo, after a deep pull at the bottle. " It seems like anythin' is liable to happen around here, but I never expected to be ambushed by a danged train."

They crawled back through the barbed-wire right-of-way fence, and headed for home, too muddled to do much wondering what it was all about.

The train passed Jim Legg before he reached Blue Wells, and he got there just after the announcement of the hold-up. A crowd had gathered at the depot, and Jim Legg heard some one saying that about thirty thousand had been stolen.

He heard some one question Chet Le Moyne, who admitted that the Santa Rita pay-roll had been on the train. Men had gone to notify the sheriff. Jim Legg did not realise that they were speaking about the train he had fell out of, even when the dishevelled express messenger made his appearance. He had been picked up along the track.

The engine crew were offering all the information they had to interested listeners.

" There were three men," said the engineer.

" Three that you saw," amended the messenger, who was nursing a black eye, several facial bruises and a bad limp. " The fourth one tangled with me in the car. That's how the door happened to be open. He got on at Encinas. I ordered him off the car and he tangled with me. In the fight we both fell off. But I sure gave him enough to make him remember me."

" Was he masked ? " some one asked.

" Masked ? No."

" What kind of a lookin' geezer ? "

" Great big son-of-a-gun. It was kinda dark in the car, and I didn't see his face very plain. I never suspected that he might be a stick-up man, or I'd have took a shot at him, but it all happened so quick that I didn't have time. He tried to pull his gun, but I blocked it, and we sure pulled some scrap."

Jim Legg kept in the background, wondering at the coincidence. Two scraps in express cars in the same evening.

" And we pretty near got 'em, even at that," said the fireman. " They jumped out of the car, leavin' me and Frank in there. Frank got the messenger's shotgun and sure sprayed 'em good and plenty.

" But they were tough eggs, and stopped to do battle. You can see where their bullets hit the car. I think we hit some of 'em. But one of their bullets split the slide jigger on the pump-gun ; so we decided to quit the battle."

Two men came panting into the crowd.

" We can't find the sheriff," they announced.

"His horses are gone from his stable; so he must be out of town."

"Aw, he couldn't find the hole in a doughnut, anyway," said one of the men.

"And his deputy is at Encinas," added one of the men who had gone after the sheriff. "We found that out at the Oasis."

"Anyway, there's no use chasin' hold-up men at night," said Le Moyne. "Nobody knows which way they went. They probably had their horses planted near where the safe was busted, and by now they're miles away. What I'd like to know is this: Who knew that the pay-roll was comin' in to-night?"

No one seemed to know the answer. Jim Legg moved in beside a man and asked him where the hold-up had taken place.

"The train that jist came in from Encinas," said the man.

"This last one?"

"There's only one a day, stranger."

Jim Legg turned away, leading Geronimo on a short piece of rope, and headed up the street, looking for a hotel.

"That messenger is the first liar I ever appreciated," he told the dog. "I'm a great big son-of-a-gun, I am, and I tried to pull a gun. I'll bet Ananias turned over in his grave to-night."

They were just passing the front of Louie Sing's restaurant when a dog shot out of the alley, followed by an empty can and a volley of Chinese expletives.

It was evident that a stray dog had been trying to steal something from the restaurant kitchen.

As quick as a flash Geronimo tore the rope from Jim's hand, and was hot on the trail of the departing dog. They disappeared in the dark, leaving Jim Legg staring after them. He waited for several minutes, but the dog did not appear. Then he went on to the one-story adobe hotel, where he secured a room. Afterwards he went back to the street, and for the first time he realised that his valise was still on that train.

He decided to try to recover it the next day. But there was no sign of Geronimo ; so Jim Legg finally went back to the hotel, hoping that the dog would return and be in evidence the next day. Jim was still a little sore from his battle in the express car, although his face and hands did not show any signs of the conflict. But he found that his body contained plenty of black-and-blue spots, and in places he had lost considerable skin.

But he ignored them, yawned widely, and fairly fell into his blankets. Mellon & Company seemed a million miles away, and years and years ago.

CHAPTER V

PAUL THE APOSTLE

THE Taylor ranch, by its brand name the Double Bar 8, was one of the old-time ranches. The ranch-house was a two-story adobe, closely resembling the Hopi in architecture, as the roof of the first story was used as a porch of the second. The bunk-house was one story, on the opposite side of the patio, and a semicircle adobe wall, three feet thick, extended from each end of the bunk-house, and circled the ranch-house. At the front was a huge gate, arched over with adobe, and at the two sides of the patio were entrances. In the centre of the patio was an old well. The stables, sheds, and corrals were at the rear of the bunk-house.

Earlier residents had planted oaks, pepper trees, and flowering eucalyptus, which had grown into big trees, shading the patio, where grape-vines clambered over the old walls, tangled with the climbing roses. From afar it appeared an oasis in the gray and purple of the hills.

It was the following day after the train robbery. Marion Taylor lifted a bucket of water from the old well and poured it into a trough, while she held the lead-rope of a blue-black horse, a tall, rangy

animal, a few degrees better bred than the average
range animal.

The girl was bareheaded, the sleeves of her white
waist rolled to her elbows. She wore a divided
skirt of brown material, and a serviceable pair of
tan riding-boots. Her hair was twisted in braids

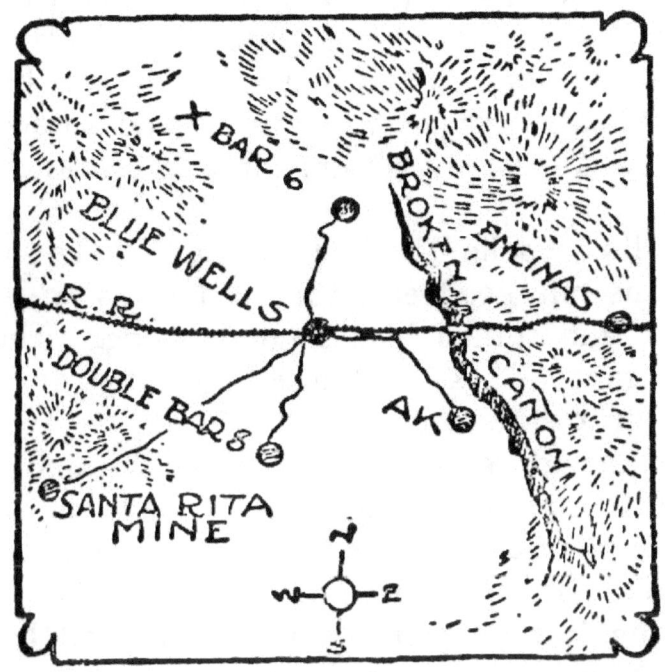

around her well-shaped head, and held in place
with a hammered silver comb set with turquoise.

She was of average height and rather slim, with
the olive tint from the desert sun. Her eyes were
wide and blue, and her well-shaped lips parted in
a smile, showing a flash of white teeth, when the
horse snorted at the splash of water in the
trough.

" Somebody must 'a' pinned yore ears back,

Spike," she said softly. " Or are yuh trying' to make me think yo're a bad horse ? "

The ears of the blue-black snapped ahead, as if he understood, and he plunged his muzzle into the clear water, drinking gustily, while the girl drew another bucket and gently poured it into the trough. A burro came poking in through the patio gate, an old ancient of the Arizona hills. His right ear had been broken and looped down over his eye, and his long, scraggly gray hair carried an accumulation of almost everything that grew and wore spines.

" Hallo, Apollo," called the girl. The burro lifted his one good ear, thrust out his whiskered muzzle, and sniffed like a pointer dog. Then he brayed raucously, shook himself violently, and came slowly up to the trough.

The horse drew aside, being either through drinking or too proud to drink with such an object. The burro looked at the horse, decided not to be particular, and proceeded to drink deeply.

Marion leaned against the curbing and laughed at the burro. That was the one reason the ancient was tolerated around the ranch—to make them laugh. His goat-like appetite was a constant provoker of profanity. Shirts, boots, straps, bedding, anything eatable or uneatable went into his maw. And as a result the inhabitants of the Double Bar 8 were careful not to leave anything lying around loose.

And Apollo was not to be tampered with. In spite of his age he was quick to resent any familiarity, and to feel the caress of his heels left nothing to be desired in the way of shocks. At one time Buck Taylor and Peeler had roped Apollo and clipped him closely, and so heavy was his coat that he almost died from chills, with the thermometer at 115 degrees in the shade.

As Marion turned away from the well and started leading the horse back toward the gate, three horsemen rode up. They were Apostle Paul, Buck, and Peeler, who had left the ranch the morning previous to search for Double Bar 8 cattle, which had been reported thirty miles away on the Yellow Horn mesa.

Marion continued out of the patio and met them just outside the gate. With them was a strange dog, which came up to her, acting very friendly. It was the missing Geronimo.

" Where did you get the dog ? " asked Marion, after greetings had been exchanged.

" He picked us up," smiled her father. " I dunno who owns him. There was a piece of rope draggin', and we took it off, 'cause it was always gettin' hung up on somethin'. Friendly cuss, ain't he."

Geronimo danced around, as if he knew what was being said about him. Apostle Paul Taylor was a tall, skinny, lean-faced man, with a hooked nose, wide mouth, and deep-set gray eyes. His hair was fast turning gray, and he stooped a trifle.

Buck Taylor was almost replica of his father, except that he was bow-legged, had a mop of brown hair, and did not stoop. The half-breed,

Peeler, was heavy-set, deep-chested, typically Indian in features, and showing little of his white blood. The two Taylors were dressed in blue calico shirts, overalls, chaps, high-heeled boots and sombreros. The half-breed's raiment was practically the same, except that he wore a faded red shirt, scarlet muffler, and his hat-band was a riot of coloured beads.

All three men wore belts and holstered guns, and in addition to this the two Taylors had rifles hung to their saddles. They were dusty, weary from their long ride. The Apostle Paul dismounted and handed his reins to Peeler.

" Did yuh find any stock on the mesa ? " asked Marion.

" About thirty head," replied her father. " Wild as hawks too. We brought 'em in as far as Buzzard Springs. Anythin' new ? "

" Not a thing, Dad."

" You ain't tried ridin' Spike, have yuh ? "

Marion shook her head and looked at the blue-black.

" Then yuh better let Buck or Peeler fork him first. He ain't been saddled for three months."

" Yeah, and the last time I climbed him he piled me quick," laughed Buck. " Let Peeler do it."

" After pay-day," grinned Peeler. " I don't want to die with money comin' to me."

" Pshaw, I'll ride him myself," said Marion.

Her father laughed and turned toward the gate when two men rode around from behind the bunk-house and came up to them. It was Scotty Olsen, the sheriff, and Al Porter, the deputy. Porter was a big man, dark-featured, with a nose entirely too large for the rest of his face, and very flat cheek-bones.

" Hyah, Sheriff," greeted Taylor.

" Howdy."

The sheriff removed his hat and bowed awkwardly to Marion,—

" Howdy, Miss Taylor."

" Hallo, Sheriff," replied the girl.

Olson rubbed a huge hand across his big moustaches. There was still a lump on his forehead, where he had bumped himself on the floor in the Oasis.

" Just gettin' in ? " queried Porter, glancing at the horses.

Apostle Paul nodded quickly.

" Yeah. Been back on Yellow Horn mesa, lookin' for cattle."

" Way up there, eh ? " said the sheriff. " Quite a ride."

" Went up yesterday," offered Buck.

" Uh-huh," the sheriff eased himself in the saddle. " Then yuh wasn't around here last night, eh ? "

" Nope. Why ? "

" Didn't yuh hear about the hold-up ? "

" Hold-up ? " Taylor shook his head. " Where ? "

" Last night," said Porter, " the train was robbed between Broken Cañon and Blue Wells. They got the Santa Rita pay-roll."

" Well, I'll be darned ! " exclaimed Taylor. " Anybody hurt ? "

" Nope."

" They must 'a' got close to thirty thousand," said Buck.

Porter turned quickly.

" What do you know about it, Buck ? "

Buck stared back at him, his eyes hardening at the implication in the deputy's question.

" I don't reckon the amount of the Santa Rita pay-roll is any secret, Porter."

" Thasso ? " Porter shrugged his shoulders.

" Yes, that's so." Buck dropped his reins and walked over to Porter, who squinted narrowly at him.

" I don't like the way yuh said that, Porter."

" The way I said what ? " queried Porter.

" You know what I mean," declared Buck angrily.

" Drop it, Buck," advised his father, and turned to Olson.

" How many men in the gang, Scotty ? "

" Three that we know of—possibly a fourth. A man got on the express car when the train stopped at Encinas, and him and the express messenger had a fight. They fell out of the door and rolled into the ditch. It kinda looks as though this feller was one of the gang. Anyway, there was three that stopped the train, cut off the engine and express car, and blowed the safe."

" Are you just startin' out after 'em ? " asked Buck, squinting at the sun. " Not very early, it seems to me."

" I didn't know nothin' about it until this

mornin'," said Porter. "I came in from Encinas early this mornin' on a freight, and went to bed. I got up jist before noon, and they told me about it ; so I got the sheriff and we started out."

Apostle Paul turned to the sheriff, whose ears were red.

"Where were you all this time, Scotty ? "

"He was in jail," said Porter.

"In jail ? "

"In my own jail," said Olson angrily. "Oyster Shell, Eskimo Swensen, and Johnny Grant came over to my office last night. They were drunk, and insisted that I had stolen their horses. And they wanted to look in the cells, the —— fools ! Jist because they was drunk I let 'em look, and they accidentally locked me in.

"I told 'em where to find the keys, but they went on out and never came back. That's why nobody could find me last night. I never knowed there was a hold-up until Porter showed up this noon. And somebody turned our horses loose, too. Mebbe it was that drunken bunch from the AK. Anyway, we're goin' over and tell 'em about it, yuh betcha."

Marion turned away, shaking with laughter, while her father and the other two of the Double Bar 8 choked back their laughter. They knew the gang from the AK very well indeed. But it was no laughing matter to the two officers.

"I can arrest them three drunks for interferin' with an officer," declared Olson hotly. "They interfered with the law when they locked me in. I was badly needed, I tell yuh."

" Sure yuh was," choked Buck. " If they hadn't locked yuh up you'd 'a' had all three of them robbers in jail now."

" Mebbe. Anyway, I'd have been on their trail."

" Where'd yuh git the new dog ? " asked Porter.

" New dog ? " queried Buck. " That one ? Huh ! We raised him."

" Never seen him before."

" Lotsa things you never seen before."

" Have yuh any clues ? " asked Apostle Paul.

" Clues ? " The sheriff wasn't sure of that word.

" Yeah—evidence that might lead yuh to the outlaws."

" We ain't had no time yet."

" Then what are yuh wastin' it around here for ? " demanded Buck.

Porter glared at Buck, but did not reply. He disliked this thin-faced young man, but was just a trifle dubious about starting anything with him.

" Well, I s'pose we might as well be goin' along," said the sheriff. " Mebbe we'll swing around and look in at the AK. I've sure got a few things to say to them fellers."

" God be with yuh, brother," said Apostle Paul piously. " The AK is sure a good place to make a talk, but when the collection is taken up, you'll find small pay for yore work."

" We'll make 'em respect the law ! " snapped Porter.

" Yes, you will," said Buck. " You better back yore law with an army. They may love yuh for startin' trouble with 'em, but they'll never respect yuh. My advice to you jiggers would be to let the AK alone. You'll never find out who robbed that train if yuh try to shove the law down the necks of them three."

" Well, I'm runnin' my own office ! " snapped Olson hotly. " No drunken puncher can lock me in my own jail and not hear about it."

" Let 'em hear about it, by all means—but in a roundabout way, Scotty. And please don't swear any more. Remember, there's ladies and gentlemen present."

" Ex-cuse me," grunted Scotty, picking up his reins. " Well, we'll be goin' along, folks. *Adios.*"

" *Adios, amigo,*" said Apostle Paul.

Porter glared at Buck, who wrinkled his nose at the big deputy, and rode away.

They watched the two riders head east across the little valley, riding side by side, as if carrying on a conversation.

" You think they ever find out who rob that train ? " asked Peeler.

Buck snorted and headed for the stable.

" Find out nothin', Peeler. Them two jiggers couldn't find their own boots. I'd like to be at the AK when they start their war-talk. That sure was funny about lockin' him in his own cell."

Peeler did not reply. He stopped at the stable door and rubbed his chin thoughtfully. Buck looked at him sharply.

" Whatsa matter, Peeler ? "

" I'm tryin' to think of one word, Buck."

" What kind of a word ? "

Peeler smiled softly.

" I think it is ' convenient.' "

" Convenient ? What for ? "

" For the robbers, Buck. That he is locked in his cell."

Buck stared at Peeler for a moment. Then :—

" Yea-a-a-a, that might be true. But it's nothin' to us, so we will forget it, eh ? "

" I forget," smiled Peeler.

Porter was very angry when he and the sheriff rode away from the Taylor ranch, heading for the AK. He was inclined to do a lot of talking, once he was far enough away to conceal his language from the Taylor family.

" I tell yuh they know somethin', Scotty."

" Do you think so, Al ? "

" Yo're right. Didn't Buck speak right up and tell how much money was in that pay-roll ? And didn't he get right on the prod when I picked him up on it ? Don't tell me that he don't know somethin' about it. They've been to Yaller Horn mesa, have they ? That's a good excuse."

" Do yuh think that's enough evidence to arrest 'em on, Al ? "

" Well, mebbe not. But it's sure enough to suspect 'em on. I wouldn't trust any of 'em as far as I could throw a bull by the tail. Buck's a bad *hombre*, Scotty. The old man is pretty salty, and that breed fits in well with the bunch."

Scotty nodded. He was in the habit of agreeing with Porter, which saved him many an argument.

" We've got to watch 'em," continued Porter. " They're slick."

" Slick," agreed Scotty absently. " I'm jist wonderin' what to say to them slick-ears at the AK."

" Give 'em ——," advised Porter. " They shore need a good curryin', Scotty."

" I know they do, Al. But they won't listen to reason. I dunno why they locked me in that jail last night."

Porter grinned sarcastically, but sobered suddenly.

" Say, Scotty, here's somethin' to think about. They locked yuh in yore cell, and in about an hour the train was held up. Does that mean anythin' to you ? "

Scotty shook his head.

" My ! Yo're dense. Listen." Porter repeated his statement. " Now do yuh get it ? "

" You mean—they locked me up and robbed the train ? "

" They locked yuh up—and the train was robbed, wasn't it ? "

" Yeah, I know that, Al; but they was too drunk."

" Acted too drunk, yuh mean."

" Well, they acted—say, Al," the sheriff grinned slowly, " you sure can see things. I wonder if that ain't right ? But it ain't enough evidence to arrest 'em on, is it ? "

" Well, mebbe not enough to arrest 'em on, but it's enough for us to suspect 'em real hard, and to keep an eye on 'em, Scotty."

" Yo're sure gittin' evidence," applauded the sheriff. " Al, I'd be lost without yuh. You think faster than I do. I'd prob'ly think of these things after a while, yuh see. And they prob'ly turned our broncs loose ; so's we couldn't foller 'em, even if I got loose."

" I was jist goin' to mention that part of it, Scotty. Yuh see how things work out."

" Yeah. You'd make a good sheriff, Al."

" Sure. Mebby I will be. Unless somethin' happens I'll take a crack at the office next election."

" Will yuh ? I dunno what I'll do. A feller gits kinda 'tached to a job like this, don'tcha know it ? Yo're prob'ly a better deputy than you'd ever be a sheriff. A feller has to have certain qualifications to be a sheriff, and it ain't as easy as it looks. Buck was kinda sore at yuh, wasn't he ? "

" Yeah, and he'll get smart jist once too often. One of these days I'm goin' to bend him plumb shut and rub his nose off agin' his knee. I'll jist stand so much from a *hombre* like him."

" You sure hang on to yore temper well, Al."

" Feller's got to, when he's a deputy. Yuh can't go fightin' every whippoorwill that wants a fight. It don't look well, Scotty."

The AK ranch was located well away from the hills, and about three miles south-east of Blue Wells. It was a typical Arizona ranch ; the buildings were part adobe, but more elaborate and larger than those of the Double Bar 8. There was no patio to the AK, but the group of buildings were fenced in with barbed wire.

The sheriff and deputy rode in through the gate and up to the ranch-house, where they met old George Bonnette, owner of the outfit. He was a pudgy little man, almost bald, almost toothless, one cheek bulged from a huge chew of tobacco. He spat explosively and nodded to the officers. It was not often that the law came to the AK, and the old man looked at them curiously.

" Howdy, George," said the sheriff.

" 'Lo, Scotty ; hyah, Porter," Bonnette shifted his chew and waited for them to state their errand.

" Where's the boys ? " asked Scotty, glancing around.

" Well," the old man scratched his head, " I've only got three workin' here now. T'day is pay-day."

" Meanin' that they've gone to town, eh ? "

" Follerin' the natcheral inclination of cow-punchers, I'd say that's where they've gone. Whatcha want 'em fer ? "

" O, nothin' much." Scotty sighed with evident relief. He really didn't want them very badly.

" You heard about the hold-up, didn't yuh ? " asked Porter.

Bonnette hadn't. And he grew so interested in Porter's recital of it that he bit off two more chews of tobacco during the telling, which swelled his cheek until one eye was almost closed.

" Well, the dern cusses ! " he said earnestly. " Thirty thousand dollars, eh. Worth takin', eh ? Who wouldn't ? Got anythin' to work on, Scotty ? "

"Well," said Scotty darkly, "we might have more'n anybody'd think, George. Did the boys find their horses?"

"Hm-m-m-m," the old man scratched his head. "Seems to me I did hear one of 'em say they walked home, and that their horses was here when they arrived. Them broncs was raised here at the AK, and they'd head for home. I didn't pay much attention, but I did hear Eskimo say that somebody turned their broncs loose in town last night."

"I jist wondered if they got 'em," said Scotty.

Bonnette squinted at Scotty, his brows lifted inquiringly.

"Didja ride all the way out here to find that out?"

"Not exactly, George. Yuh see, them three jaspers locked me in my own jail last night. Didja know that?"

"In yore own jail? No, I didn't know it, Scotty."

"Yeah, they did, George. And I was in there when word came of the robbery, and didn't know a thing about it. They're liable for blockin' the law."

"Yeah, I s'pose they are. Huh!" Bonnette turned away, choking a trifle, and when he turned back there were tears in his eyes.

"We came down here to see about it," said Porter. "It's a —— of a note, when things like that happen, Bonnette. Them three fellers ort to be run out of the country."

"Yea-a-ah?" The old man looked narrowly at

Porter. " Why don't yuh go ahead and do it, Porter. They're all of age, yuh know. And there ain't a milk drinker in the crowd ; so they really wouldn't suffer if yuh took 'em away from the cows."

" Oh, they ain't so tough," retorted Porter. " They're not runnin' this country. They've kinda had their own way in Blue Wells for a long time, but now is the time to call a halt. We're civilised, I'll tell yuh that."

" What do yuh mean, Porter ? "

" Well, all of us—ain't we ? "

" I dunno. Sometimes I wonder if we are. We ain't savages. We don't worship no idols, nor we don't eat each other. Holdin' up a train is a sign of civilisation. I dunno about lockin' a sheriff in his cell. It sure ain't old-fashioned, 'cause I never heard of it bein' done before."

" Well, I don't care a —— ! " snorted the sheriff. " They done it to me, and I'm sure goin' to let 'em know that I'm sore about it."

" Yo're probably more interested in that than yuh are in findin' the men who held up the train."

" Yuh think so, do yuh ? " growled Porter. " Well, I'll tell yuh we're plenty interested in that, too. C'mon, Scotty ; we're jist wastin' time around here."

" You don't need to get mad at me," laughed Bonnette. " I never locked up any sheriffs."

" Well, yore men did ! " snapped Scotty.

Bonnette laughed at the sheriff's red face.

" I'll prob'ly fire 'em for not havin' more respect for the law."

" Aw, c'mon," urged Porter. " We've got work to do."

They rode away from the AK, heading back toward Blue Wells, no better off for their long ride to the AK.

" I've jist been thinkin' that folks around here don't show a lot of respect for the law," said Scotty Olson.

" Well," growled Porter, " it's up to us to make 'em. I'm all through lettin' folks make remarks to me. From now on I'm goin' to make these smart pelicans set up and salute when the law shows up.":

CHAPTER VI

THE MAKING OF A COWBOY

Jim Legg awoke to a different world from what he had ever seen. Blue Wells was so typically south-western, being one long street of one and two-story adobe houses, some of them half adobe, half frame. There were no sidewalks, no lawns, no shrubbery. The fronts of the buildings were unpainted, and the signs were so scoured from wind and sand that the letters were barely legible.

No one seemed to pay any attention to Jim Legg. The town was full of cattlemen, and the topic of conversation was the train robbery. Jim Legg listened to the different ideas on the subject, no two of which were alike. He realised that if he and the express messenger had not fought and fell out of the car, they would have been in the centre of things.

And Jim Legg was glad the messenger had lied about the physical proportions of the man who had attacked him. Jim wondered what had become of Geronimo, but did not ask any one. And then Jim Legg ran into the three men from the AK outfit. Their pockets were lined with a month's pay, and they were happily inclined toward all humanity.

Oyster Shell, backed against the Oasis bar, was the first to see Jim Legg. His eyes opened wide and he spurred Johnny Grant on the calf of his left leg.

"Johnny," he said softly, " do m'eyes deceive me ?"

Johnny looked upon Jim Legg with much the same expression that a scientist might exhibit upon finding the fossil egg of a dinosaur.

" Welcome," said Johnny. " I welcome you to Blue Wells."

" How do you do ? " smiled Jim. " Nice day, isn't it ? "

" Yeah," said Johnny. " We have one like this every thirty days. What grade of poison does yore stummick stand ? "

Jim Legg had never drank anything more potent than a small glass of beer, but he knew that he was now in Rome, so he said :—

" Oh, anything you gentlemen are drinking."

" Hooch ! " exclaimed Eskimo, and the busy bartender sent the bottle spinning down the bar, followed by four glasses.

" You want a wash ? " asked Johnny, meaning a glass of water or soda.

Jim Legg glanced at his hands and looked at himself in the back-bar.

" No," he said finally. " I don't think so."

The three cowpunchers exchanged quick glances. Fate had sent them something to play with. Eskimo poured out a full glass for their new playmate, who almost strangled over it. But he got it down.

" That's liquor," declared Johnny, smacking his lips.

" It's gug-good," whispered Jim Legg.

He cleared his throat and wondered at the warm glow within him.

" I'm buyin'," declared Oyster, spinning a dollar on the bar, which got them four clean glasses.

Again Jim Legg managed to swallow the liquor, but this time it did not strangle him. He laughed gleefully at nothing in particular and rested a hand on Johnny Grant's shoulder.

" My name's Legg," he told them. " Jim Legg."

" That's quite a name," agreed Johnny. " My name's Grant, this one's name is Shell, and that Jewish friend of ours there is named Swensen. We're Johnny, Oyster, and Eskimo respectably."

They all shook hands gravely.

" If the clerk will furnish us with clean glasses, I'll make a purchase," said Jim Legg solemnly.

" My —— ! " exclaimed Eskimo explosively.

" Just why ? " queried Jim Legg.

" I thought my belt was comin' off."

They filled their glasses and drank heartily. By this time Jim Legg seemed to be getting numb, but happily so. The world was bathed in a rosy glow, and he wanted to sing and dance.

" Jist what is yore business, Misser Legg ? " asked Oyster.

" I came here," said Jim. " to be a cowpuncher."

Johnny Grant's foot slipped, and he sat down heavily on the bar-rail.

" That," said Eskimo, owlishly-wise, " is a

ambitious thing for to become. I'll betcha yuh came to the right place, Jim."

"I—I——" Jim hesitated because his tongue did not seem to exactly function. "I picked thish place at ra-ra-random."

"That shounds like a college yell," said Oyster.

"You can't be no cowpuncher in them clothes," explained Eskimo. "Never, nossir. You look like Sunday. But in the proper clothes you'd be a dinger."

"I intend to dresh the part," said Jim thickly. "Perhaps I can secure the proper dresh here in Blue Wells."

"Oh, you can," said Johnny. "We can take you to a place where you can buy just what yuh need, pervidin' you've got the *dinero*."

"*Dinero?*"

"Money."

"I've got five hundred dollars."

"My!" Johnny took off his hat. "And you want to be a cowpuncher—with five hundred dollars!"

"Isn't it enough?"

"Don' nobody speak for a moment," begged Oyster. "I want to conchentrate. I'm about to go into a tranch."

"Sh-h-h-h-h!" warned Johnny. "The man is looking into the future."

"Is he a medium?" asked Jim Legg, owl-eyed, as he stared at Oyster.

"Medium! He's rare," chuckled Eskimo.

" I shee shomethin' comin' to a man named Jim Legg," stated Oyster, his eyes closed tightly.

" Yuh see ? " applauded Johnny.

" Yessir," nodded Jim. " Maybe we better let him alone, while we get me shome clothes."

" He's comin' out of it," announced Eskimo.

Oyster's face twitched convulsively and his eyes opened.

" Where is the haberdasher's ? " asked Jim Legg.

The three cowboys stared owlishly at each other.

" Oh, them folks," Johnny Grant squinted thoughtfully.

" Must 'a' been that German fambly that nested in down on the forks of the Rio Creek," said Eskimo. " They're gone. Let's go buy somethin' to make a real, regular cowboy out of this here, now, Jimmy Limbs."

. . . . . .

The sheriff and deputy came back to Blue Wells in bad humour. They stabled their horses and went to the office. Scotty Olson leaned against the doorway and looked across the street at the horses tied at the Oasis hitch-rack. The three at the far end were from the AK ; a tall roan, a sorrel, and a gray.

Al Porter sagged back in a chair, placed his feet on top of the desk, and drew his sombrero down over his eyes.

" If I was you I'd go over to the Oasis and have a talk with them AK scoundrels," he told Scotty. " If I was sheriff of this county I'd shore impress upon 'em that this is a dignified office. I'd make it dignified, y'betcha."

Scotty turned troubled eyes upon his deputy.

" You would ! You'll sag jist as quick as anybody, when it comes to trouble. All the way back from the AK you've told me what you'd do. Talk ! Yeah, you can talk, Al. If talkin' was worth anything, you'd be President of the U.S.A."

" A-a-a-a-aw, —— ! " yawned Porter. " Don't try to pass the buck to me, feller. It ain't my trouble. If you want to forgive 'em for lockin' yuh in a cell—go ahead. It's none of my business, anyway. But if yuh want to know what I'd do, I'll——"

" I don't ! —— it, Al, I don't care to hear what you'd do—unless yo're willin' to tell the truth."

" All right. We'll just drop the subject. But if they locked me in a——"

" They didn't ! Al, I wish they had ! I'd throw away the keys and leave yuh there until yuh quit runnin' off at the mouth. I'm more interested in that train robbery than I am in the AK cowpunchers."

" Yeah, and you stand a fine chance of catchin' em, Scotty. They've had a danged long start of us by this time."

" I s'pose."

Scotty leaned back against the door and studied the street. He saw Tex Alden ride in and tie his horse at the rack beside the three AK horses.

" Tex Alden jist rode in," he said indifferently.

" Thasso ? " It did not seem to interest Porter.

" Probably came in to lose some more money."

" Lost eight thousand to Antelope Neal yesterday," said Porter. " Wonder where he got so much money. He don't own that X Bar 6."

" Don't he ? "

" He sure don't. It belongs to an Eastern outfit."

" Well, I don't care," said Scotty.

He had enough worries of his own to think about. He smoothed his buffalo-horn moustache and almost wished he weren't the sheriff of Blue Wells.

Tex Alden left his horse and started across the street toward a store when Lee Barnhardt called to him from the door of his office. Tex turned and went over to the door of the lawyer's office, where Barnhardt was standing.

" I just wondered if you wasn't coming to see me, Tex," smiled Barnhardt.

The big cowboy blinked, wondering just why he should make it a point to see Barnhardt that day.

" Why, I dunno," he faltered. " Hadn't thought of it, Lee."

The lawyer motioned Tex into the office and closed the door. He sat down at his desk, filled his pipe carefully, scratched a match on the sole of his shoe, and puffed explosively. Then he sagged back in his chair and looked at Tex with an approving grin.

" I'll give you credit for a clean job, Tex," he said, lowering his voice confidentially. " A —— clean job."

" Yeah ? " Tex scratched his chin. " Just what is it, Lee ? "

"What is it?" The lawyer leaned forward, the smoke curling lazily from his nostrils. "Oh, now, Tex! We're friends, you know."

"All right," grinned Tex. "And what am I supposed to say?"

"It isn't what you say—it's what you do. My mouth is shut tight, except between us, Tex. And don't forget that I was the one who told you where to get it."

The big cowboy studied Lee Barnhardt, a puzzled frown between his brows.

"Go ahead and talk about it, Lee," he said.

Barnhardt's shrewd eyes appraised the foreman of the X Bar 6. He knew Tex was not a man you could scare or drive. He would have to go easy, at least until he knew just what Tex meant to do. Then——

"You owe me eight thousand dollars, Tex," he said.

"And a swell chance you've got of collectin' it."

"Oh, I dunno, Tex. Anyway, I'll be satisfied with the eight thousand. It ought to be more, but I can take the eight thousand with a clear conscience, because I'm not supposed to know where it comes from."

"Would yuh mind repeatin' that?" asked Tex evenly.

"No need of that, Tex. You know what I mean. There were two or three men with you last night. I realise that they have to get their share, but even at that—well, as I said before, I'll take the eight thousand and call it square."

Tex got to his feet and walked back to the door, where he turned and looked at Barnhardt, who had also stood up, leaning across his desk.

" I reckon you've gone loco, Lee," he said softly. " I dunno what yo're talkin' about—and I don't reckon you do either."

" The —— I don't," rasped the lawyer. " If you think you can cut me out of that Santa Rita pay-roll, you're crazy. It was done on my information, and you'll come clean with me, or you'll find just how high a fee I can charge."

Tex blinked at him, a puzzled expression in his eyes. Then he turned on his heel and left the office, while Barnhardt stopped at the window and watched Tex walk slowly across the street to the Oasis, where he stopped and glanced back towards the office, before going into the saloon.

Barnhardt was mad. In fact, he was almost mad enough to go to the sheriff and tell him that Tex Alden knew that the Santa Rita pay-roll was coming in on that train. But he was not quite mad enough to do that. There would be plenty of time for that, in case Tex could not be induced to make a split.

Barnhardt put on his hat, yanked it down on his head, forcing his ears to flare out, and headed for the sheriff's office, intending to find out what the sheriff had in mind.

He was nearing the Blue Wells General Merchandise Store entrance, when four men came out. Three of them were the boys from the AK, but the fourth one was a stranger. Every article of his apparel shrieked of newness.

His sombrero was the biggest they could find in town, and was surmounted with a silver-studded band. His robin's-egg-blue shirt was of flimsy silk, his overalls new ; and the creaking bat-wing chaps were hand-stamped and silver-ornamented. His thin neck was circled with a scarlet silk muffler, and his feet were encased in the highest-heeled boots in town.

Around his waist was a wide yellow cartridge belt, glistening with its load of cartridges, and the revolver holster was a sample of leather-working art. He carried a heavy Colt .45 in his hand—or rather in both hands. James Eaton Legg was in a fair way to become a cowpuncher.

Barnhardt stopped and looked at him. It did not require an expert eye to detect that all four of them were pie-eyed drunk. Barnhardt noticed that the sheriff was coming up the street from his office. The lawyer had heard about what had happened to the sheriff, and he wondered just what the sheriff would have to say to the boys from the AK.

Eskimo stepped back from Jim Legg, reared back on his heels, and looked the young man over with appraising eyes.

"Jimmie," he said thickly, "yo're a cowboy. Yessir, if you ain't, I've never seen one. Yuh hurt m' eyes."

"Look at 'm slaunch-wise," advised Johnny Grant. "Don't never take a chance of lookin' at him square. Ain't he a work of art ? Whatcha tryin' to do with that gun ? "

Jim Legg was trying to see how the thing functioned, and it was fully loaded. It was the first time he had ever handled a six-shooter, and it interested him.

" Don't cock it ! " choked Eskimo. " Yeah— that thing yuh jist pulled back ! Don't touch that thing underneath it ! Keep yore finger off it, I tell yuh ! A-a-a-w, Johnny, take it away from him, can'tcha ? "

" Aw, whazzamatter ? " grunted Jim Legg. " I'd like to shee shomebody take it away from me."

" No-o-o-o-o ! " wailed Johnny, ducking aside. " Point it in the air, you cross between a monkey and a Christmas tree ! "

But Jim Legg reeled around on his high-heels, giggling drunkenly, the big gun in both hands.

" Don't do that, you —— fool ! " wailed Oyster. " Aw, fer——"

Wham ! The big gun spouted smoke between Johnny Grant and Eskimo, who promptly fell side-ways, and the bullet tore into the dirt almost under the feet of the sheriff, who had stopped about fifty feet away.

The recoil of the gun caused Jim Legg to turn half-way around. He staggered back on his heels, possibly more frightened than any of the rest.

" Whee-e-e-e-e ! " he yelled, and his next shot missed Lee Barnhardt by a full inch.

" Yee-e-e-e-o-o-ow ! " screamed Johnny Grant. " Cowboy blood ! Look at the sheriff ! "

Scotty Olson was galloping back toward his office, his legs working as fast as possible, his hat clutched tightly in one hand.

" Look at the lawyer ! " yelled Eskimo, and they turned to see Lee Barnhardt go head first into his office door, like a frightened gopher, dodging a hawk.

But Oyster Shell was not paying any attention to the departing sheriff and lawyer. He wrenched the gun from Jim's hands and grasped Jim by the arm.

" C'mon, you —— fools ! " he yelled. " The sheriff don't know it was an accident, and we don't want to lose Jimmy ! "

Realising that Oyster was right, the other two helped him rush the bewildered Jim across the street to the hitch-rack.

" Git on ! " snorted Oyster, whirling his gray horse around. " Git in the saddle, Jim ; I'll ride behind."

" I never rode no horsh." Jim drew back, shaking his head.

" You never shot at no sheriff before either ! " snapped Eskimo.

He swung Jim Legg up bodily and fairly threw him into the saddle. Jim managed to grasp the horn in time to prevent himself from going off the other side.

The others were mounting in a whirl of dust. Jim felt Oyster swing up behind him, and then he seemed to lose all sense of direction. The gray flung down its head and went pitching down the street, trying to rid itself of the unaccustomed load, while on either side rode Eskimo and Johnny, yelling at the top of their voices.

" Pull leather, you ornyment ! " yelled Johnny. " Anchor yoreself, son ! You'll either be a cow-puncher or a corpse ! "

After about ten or twelve lurching bucks, which did not seem to disturb Oyster to any great extent, the gray's head came up and they went out of Blue Wells like three racers on the stretch.

Scotty Olson skidded into his office, fell over a chair, and sat there, his mouth wide open, while Al Porter ran to the door in time to see the four men cross the street. He turned back to the sheriff.

" What in —— happened, Scotty ? "

Scotty got to his feet and brushed off his knees. Then he went to the corner behind his desk and picked up a double-barrelled shotgun. Breaking it open to see whether it was loaded, he limped back to the doorway in time to see the three horses go pounding out of town in a flurry of dust.

" Goin' duck huntin' ? " asked Porter sarcasti-cally.

Scotty limped back and stood the gun in the corner.

" That makes me mad," he said seriously. " I seen them AK fellers up by the store ; so I goes up there to have a heart-to-heart talk with 'em. But before I get there, one of 'em takes a shot at me and almost knocked a hole in my right boot.

And when I turned around they took another shot at me."

" That don't sound reasonable," said Porter.

" I don't give a —— how it sounds ; I was there, wasn't I ? "

The shots had attracted some attention, and the sudden exit of the AK boys made things look suspicious. Scotty and Porter went up the street, where several men had gathered in front of the store, and were talking with Lee Barnhardt, who was telling them all about it.

" I tell you, it was deliberate," he said. " I saw that cowboy take aim at me. Why, I heard that bullet sing past my ear, so close that the air from it staggered me."

" Why did he shoot at you, Lee ? " asked the storekeeper, Abe Moon, a tall, serious, tobacco-chewing person.

"I don't know. Why, I don't even know the man."

" I never seen him before either," declared the merchant. " He came in a while ago with Oyster, Eskimo, and Johnny. They were all pretty full, I think. Anyway, they outfitted this young man with everything. Even bought a six-gun, and loaded it for him. He left his other clothes, wrapped up, in the back room."

The sheriff moved in closer.

" Wasn't it one of the AK boys that done the shootin', Lee ? "

" No."

" The stranger," said one of the men. " Did yuh hear his name, Abe ? "

" They introduced him to me. Said his name was Legg."

" Legg ? " queried Barnhardt blankly. He shook his head slowly. " I dunno anybody by that name."

" I don't either—and he shot at me," said the sheriff.

" He's prob'ly one of them peculiar jiggers that would rather shoot strangers than acquaintances," said the merchant dryly.

" Well, he's goin' to hear from me," declared the sheriff.

" Write him a letter," grinned one of the men in the crowd.

" He was pretty drunk," offered the merchant.

" He wasn't too drunk to shoot straight," said Scotty. " I'm promisin' yuh right now that the next time that AK outfit comes to Blue Wells, I'm packin' a riot gun. Blue Wells has stood all it's ever goin' to from that layout. And," he added, " I don't care who knows it."

Lee Barnhardt turned on his heel and walked back to his office. Chet Le Moyne and Dug Haley, the man who had come with Le Moyne to guard the Santa Rita pay-roll, rode in and drew up in front of the store. Haley was a heavy-set, stolid looking person, with a wispy moustache and only a faint suggestion of ever having had eyebrows.

Le Moyne smiled and spoke to the men, but Haley merely nodded.

" I wanted to see you, Scotty," said Le Moyne. " Goin' back to your office pretty soon ? "

" Right away, Le Moyne."

Le Moyne nodded and rode beside the sheriff down to the office, while Haley tied his horse in front of the store, and went in to make some purchases. Le Moyne tied his horse and went into the office with the sheriff.

" What do you know, Scotty ? " asked Le Moyne.

" Not very much. It kinda looks to me as though they had a big start on us, Le Moyne."

" Have you anything to work on ? "

" I said I didn't have much." Scotty wasn't going to tell Le Moyne of his suspicions against the Taylors or the AK.

" Uh-huh," muttered Le Moyne. " Well, I just wanted to tell you that the express company will have a man on the job, and the Santa Rita company will also have an investigator. They'll be here to-night, and I want you to help 'em all you can. We're offering a thousand dollars reward, and the express company will probably offer somethin'. What was all this stuff about you bein' locked in your own jail ? "

The sheriff told Le Moyne of the incident, and the handsome paymaster could not suppress a laugh.

" Go ahead and laugh," sighed the harassed sheriff. " It sounds funny."

" But why did they do it, Sheriff ? "

" That's somethin' I'm goin' to try and find out."

" Meanin' what ? "

" Well, it kept me from quick action on that robbery, didn't it ? "

" It rather looks that way," admitted Le Moyne.
" Well, I've got to be moving along. I just wanted
to tell you about the detectives, and I know you'll
help them all yuh can."

Le Moyne left the office and went up to the store,
where he joined Haley. Tex Alden came in to
purchase some tobacco. He nodded to Le Moyne,
made his purchases, and went out again. There
had never been open enmity between them, nor
had they ever been friends.

" Tex got hit pretty hard the other day," offered
the storekeeper. " Yuh heard about Antelope
Neal takin' eight thousand away from Tex in a
two-handed poker game, didn't yuh ? "

" I heard he did," nodded Le Moyne. " It
sounded fishy."

" Well, it wasn't. He lost it all right. What's
new on the pay-roll robbery ? "

" Not a thing. The express company has a
detective on the case, and we've sent for one. They
might find out somethin', but I doubt it. Those
men had a good start, and it's pretty hard to
identify gold coin. If they're ever caught, it
won't be through anything developed around
here."

" What do yuh think about that feller throwin'
the messenger out of the car ? That sounds funny
to me."

" It does sound rather queer," admitted Le
Moyne. " But I guess it happened. The messenger
sure looked as though he had been through a fight.
And he wasn't there when the robbery took place.

it seems. Anyway, the money is gone. We better get the mail, Jud, and head for the mine."

" How much was in that pay-roll ? " asked the merchant.

" Thirty-one thousand and eighty dollars, all in gold. It'll make somebody happy, Abe."

" Yes—or unhappy, Chet. I don't reckon any man ever got a lot of happiness from what he stole. It's unlucky money."

CHAPTER VII

JIMMY WINS HIS SPURS

'A FEW short days wrought a great change in Jim Legg. His face had received its baptism of Arizona sun, and no longer was he the pale-faced city dweller. His skin was beginning to peel, and as Johnny Grant said :—

" He peels off like a package of cigarette papers."

His hands were seared from fast-travelling ropes, his silken shirt was minus half of one sleeve, and had a huge rent down the back. His ornate sombrero had fallen off in a corral, where a circling remuda had trampled it into the sand, giving it an antique air.

And out of self-defence he had quit wearing glasses. Just now he leaned against the corral fence, trying to roll a cigarette with cramped fingers. Beside him squatted Johnny Grant, his eyes fixed curiously upon this young man, whose eyes were filled with determination.

About fifty feet away from them were Oyster and Eskimo, saddling a horse. The animal was humped painfully, squirming uneasily under the pull of the cinch, but fearing to move, because a heavy bandage had been fastened across its eyes. The two cowboys were talking softly to each other.

" This has gone past the funny stage," Johnny Grant spoke to Jimmy Legg seriously. " We was jokin' when we dared yuh to ride Cowcatcher. You can't ride him. He ditched Eskimo in four jumps, and Eskimo is the best there is around here, Jimmy."

" I said I'd ride him," reminded Jimmy Legg. " I haven't quit yet, have I ? "

Johnny Grant shook his head.

" That's why I hate to see yuh fork that bronc, Jimmy. I don't *sabe* yuh, kid. You ain't strong. Yore body ain't built for the shocks yuh get in this business. We was raised for this kinda stuff. You ain't no youngster. That bronc will jist about flatten yuh for life—and whatsa use ? "

" Johnny, I want to be a cowboy," said Jimmy seriously. " It's something I can't explain right now. I appreciate you trying to save me. I've been thrown five times since I came here, and I'm still able to hobble around."

" Yeah, I know. But this is a *horse*. He's plumb bad. If there's any slip in the boys bein' able to herd him away after he's spilled yuh, he might tromp yuh."

" But," Jim Legg spoke softly, " I've got confidence in Oyster and Eskimo. They'll do their part. If I can ride Cowcatcher, will you admit that I can ride ? "

Johnny smiled softly.

" I'll admit that yo're the best rider in the Blue Wells country."

" All set ! " called Eskimo. " Johnny, you pull the blind, after me and Oyster get all set, will yuh ? "

Johnny held Cowcatcher while Jim Legg mounted. The rough-coated gray outlaw, which had defied the best riders of the Blue Wells ranges, stiffened slightly, but did not move. Oyster and Eskimo mounted and rode in on each side of him, prepared to block the bucker from heading into obstacles, and to herd him away from the rider, in case of a spill.

They did not see the sheriff, deputy, and another rider swing around the corner of the corral and come toward them.

Jim Legg straightened up in his saddle, grasped the reins tightly, and nodded to Johnny Grant.

Johnny reached up and grasped the bandage.

" Pull leather, Jimmy," he said softly. " Don't be ashamed to do it. It's only fools and contest riders that don't, when they feel themselves goin'."

But Jim Legg shut his lips tightly and looked straight ahead. He had asked to ride Cowcatcher, after every half-way bucker on the AK had thrown him, and he was going to ride him, or get thrown clean.

Then the bandage was jerked off, and Cowcatcher was moving as he caught his first flash of sunlight, but not ahead, as they expected. Veteran of many battles, he hated the horses and riders which crowded him too closely ; so he had whirled free of them, catching them flat-footed, headed the wrong way.

Although Jim Legg was not unseated, he was flung sideways, and his right spur hooked wickedly into Cowcatcher's flank ; hooked in while the outlaw was still in the air, heading for the three riders which were not over a hundred feet away, just drawing up to witness the sport.

There was no chance for Oyster and Eskimo to ride herd on Cowcatcher. The gray outlaw churned into the dust, fairly screaming with rage, head down, running like a streak, forgetting to buck, because of that spur, socked to the full limit of the rowels into his flank.

Johnny Grant ran toward the corral, trying to see through the cloud of dust. Jim Legg was still in the same position, hands flung up, as if fearful of making a mistake and pulling leather.

The sheriff's party tried to spur their horses aside, but their slow-moving mounts failed to move quickly enough.

Came the crash of impact, the scream of a horse. A man yelled. Eskimo and Oyster were riding toward them as fast as possible, while Johnny Grant ran through the dust, trying to see what had happened.

He saw one horse and rider heading toward the ranch-house, and a moment later he heard something crash into the corral fence. Two horses were down. A gust of wind blew the dust aside, and he saw Scotty Olson on his hands and knees about twenty feet away from his horse, going around and around, like a pup trying to lie down.

Al Porter was flat on his back just beyond the two horses, which were trying to get up, and up by the house was the third member of the sheriff's party, trying to recover his reins, which he had dropped.

And there was Cowcatcher, standing in an angle of the corral fence, head hanging down, a most dejected-looking outlaw, while still on his back was Jimmy Legg, his hands resting on the saddle-horn, apparently oblivious to everything.

He slowly climbed down and staggered toward Johnny Grant, his lips parting in a foolish smile, as he whispered :—

" My ——, wasn't that a wreck ! "

Oyster and Eskimo had helped Al Porter to his feet, and he was clinging to them, puffing heavily. The sheriff managed to get up without further difficulty, and they waited for him to recover his speech. The two horses scrambled to their feet and moved toward the ranch-house, still frightened.

The sheriff was mad ; so much so, in fact, that he almost yanked one side of his moustache off, trying to find words with which to express his feelings.

" Yuh know, Sheriff," said Johnny Grant, anticipating the sheriff's coming flood of profanity, " you know it was an accident."

" Yea-a-a-huh ? " blurted the sheriff.

" Wh-wh-who was ridin' that bub-bucker ? " stammered Al Porter.

Johnny looked around at Jim Legg, who was still a trifle dazed over it all. Johnny grasped him by the arm and turned to the deputy.

" This is Jimmy Legg, the only man that ever stayed on Cowcatcher."

" I don't give a ——! " roared the sheriff. " Every time I get in sight of you fellers, somethin' happens. I'm sick and tired of it ! Do yuh hear me ? "

" Louder and more profane," begged Eskimo, cupping one hand beside his ear.

" A-a-a-aw, shut up ! " The sheriff was too mad to say anything more.

The stranger had ridden up closer to them, and was listening with an amused smile. He was a well-dressed, middle-aged sort of person, rather hard-faced.

" I got out of that pretty lucky," he said. " I happened to be just outside the crash."

" Well, I didn't," said Porter ruefully. " Any old time there's a crash—I'm in it. Boys," he turned to Johnny Grant, " this is Mr. Wade, the detective for the express company."

The boys of the AK looked Wade over critically, but the keen scrutiny of these sons of the range did not embarrass Wade. He was what is known as " hard-boiled."

" Hyah," nodded Johnny Grant. " What do yuh know ? "

" Not very much," admitted Wade. " What do you know ? "

> " I know m' head,
> I know m' feet,
> I know you'll soon
> Stand up to eat."

Oyster Shell chanted it softly, noticing that the detective was sitting rather sideways in the saddle. Wade grinned widely.

"I guess that's right," he said. "I'm not used to riding."

"You workin' on that train robbery?" asked Eskimo.

"Yes, I'm suppose to be," he turned and looked at Jimmy Legg, who was still leaning against Johnny Grant. "They tell me you're a stranger around here, Mr. Legg."

"I—I've been here a while," stammered Jimmy Legg.

"Uh-huh," nodded the sheriff, breaking in on the detective. "You showed up the night of the robbery, didn't yuh?"

"He did not," said Johnny Grant quickly, "he was here the day before."

"Here at the AK?" queried Porter.

"Yeah," defiantly.

"That's funny," smiled Porter. "We just met George Bonnette in Blue Wells, and he said you came here to the ranch the day after the hold-up. And that yuh wasn't even hired yet."

"And that none of the boys knew yuh, until they met yuh that day in Blue Wells," added Scotty Olson. "Yuh bought all yore clothes there in Blue Wells, and you near killed me and Lee Barnhardt, because yuh acted like yuh didn't know nothin' about a six-gun. And yuh had plenty of money to buy anythin' yuh wanted."

Johnny Grant, caught in a lie, did not back up an inch. He stepped in front of Jimmy Legg and glared at the sheriff.

"Well, what if he did?" demanded Johnny.

" It's nothing to quarrel about," interposed the detective. " I merely wanted to know when, how, and why he came to Blue Wells. He's a stranger around here, it seems."

" And if he is—what about it ? " asked Eskimo. " There's no law against a stranger comin' here, is there ? "

" Not at all," smiled the detective. " This man does not fit the description of any of the robbers, but we can't afford to miss any lead that might set us on the right track. There's a man and a dog to be accounted for.

" It seems that this man shipped his dog in the express car. We have a fairly accurate description of the dog, but not of the man. The express messenger fought with a man who got on his car at Encinas. They fell out of the car, while the train was in motion.

" This dog was on the car at that time, because the engineer and fireman saw him when the three robbers led them back to the car. The dog was there when the engineer got the messenger's shotgun and started battle with the three robbers.

" A few minutes later the engine crew sneaked back to their engine to escape the bullets of the bandits. The fireman says he thought he heard a man walk past the engine, just before they started back to pick up the rest of the train, but he is not sure. At any rate, the dog was missing when the train came to Blue Wells.

" Our theory is that the dog was merely a blind to let the man into the car at Encinas. It gave the robbers an inside man, in case the messenger might refuse to open the door. Of course they could dynamite the door, but that takes time. Perhaps the inside man did not expect the messenger to put up a battle, and that the falling out of the express car was an unexpected incident.

" The messenger states that the man tried to pull a gun, which strengthens the theory of the fourth bandit. It is just barely possible that this dog might be identified ; so the owner took a chance, sneaked back to the hold-up and secured the dog. This would make it appear that they felt it necessary to have the dog in their possession. That dog was in the car when the engineer and fireman went back to the engine. When the train arrived at Blue Wells, the dog was gone."

" Which don't prove anythin'," said Johnny Grant. " When the train was robbed there were three masked men on the car, and when the train got to Blue Wells there wasn't a masked man on it."

The detective laughed.

" That's true. But it doesn't explain when and how Mr. Legg came to Blue Wells."

" I walked," declared Jimmy Legg bravely. " The train passed me."

" Where ? " asked the sheriff.

" I don't know. It was dark, and I'm not familiar with this country. I got a room at a hotel that night."

" When did you hear that there had been a hold-up ? "

" I heard them talking about it the next day,"
said Jimmy Legg truthfully.

He did not think it necessary to tell them he had
also heard it the night before.

" I don't think he knows anything about it,"
said the sheriff. " He don't fit the description of
any one of the robbers, and it's a cinch he ain't
the big geezer that fought the messenger."

" What kind of a dog was it ? " asked Oyster.

" No special breed," replied the detective. " It
was of medium size, yellowish-red, and had one
black eye. At least that's the description which
was given to me."

A few minutes later the three officers rode away,
and the cowboys turned their attention to Cowcatcher, the gray outlaw, which was still beside
the corral fence. The collision with the other two
horses had wrenched its right shoulder, which
accounted for its not going any farther.

They took off the saddle and turned it loose.
The boys were loud in their praise of Jimmy's
ability as a rider. The marvel of it all was the
fact that Jim had stayed with the horse.

" If he knowed anythin' about ridin', he'd 'a'
been killed," Eskimo told Johnny a few minutes
later, after Jim had gone into the bunk-house.
" He had the luck of a drunk. I'm glad it happened
thataway, instead of havin' to pick him up on a
shovel."

" Sure," grinned Johnny, and then confidentially :
" Eskimo, I don't *sabe* that feller. Remember when
them fellers were shootin' at us from the express

car ? Remember the feller we seen, who comes along the track and gets into the car ? "

" Yeah, I remember, Johnny. But I was too drunk to remember much more than that."

" I wasn't as sober as a judge myself, Eskimo. But I'll be danged if it was a big man. Do yuh remember somethin' about somebody named Geronimo ? "

" That's right, Johnny ! I wonder if it was the man's name, or the dog's."

" And that man headed for Blue Wells, Eskimo." Eskimo nodded seriously.

" That's right. By golly, don'tcha know," Eskimo scratched his head thoughtfully, " I'm wonderin' what our little friend knows about that hold-up."

" And why he wants to be a cowboy. Anyway," Johnny grinned widely, " I'm for him. He's got guts. If the Old Man will hire him, we'll make a puncher out of him."

Jimmy Legg was thanking his stars that Geronimo had deserted him. He was stiff and sore from his efforts to learn the cattle business all in a few days, and he did not realise that the boys had been trying to make him quit. He had been thrown from bucking horses until it seemed to him that ranch life consisted of dull thuds.

Because he could not rope from a horse the boys had let him work from the ground during a day's calf-branding, and his hands were seared so badly he could hardly shut them. He had managed to make enough good casts to encourage him, and he had spent hours alone in the corral, throwing loops at a snubbing post.

But his unfailing good-humour and earnest endeavour had caused the boys to go easier than they would have had he not been so foolishly innocent. George Bonnette had watched him, but said nothing. He was not running a school for making cowpunchers, but decided that Jimmy Legg was earning his board and keep.

Jimmy had decided to ride to Blue Wells that afternoon, but after a nap, which left him stiff and sore, he decided to saddle a horse and go for a ride into the hills. The other boys had ridden away before Jimmy awoke; so he saddled the horse alone for the first time. It was a fairly well broken roan mare, and he had little difficulty. He buckled on his gun and rode away.

Although the hills were fairly open, Jimmy watched his landmarks carefully. He realised that the hills and dales looked pretty much alike, and it might be difficult for him to hit a straight line back to the ranch.

A coyote crossed in front of him, stopped long enough to get a good look, and went on. Jimmy did not realise that it was a wild animal. A flock of blue quail whirred up in front of the horse and went careering down across a brushy draw. Something told him that these were game birds, and he wondered whether they were prairie chickens. He had heard of them.

He wasted several cigarette-papers, trying to master the art of rolling a cigarette on a moving horse. He did not in the least resemble the James Eaton Legg who had slid off his high stool in Mellon & Company's office a short time before. His face was just as thin, but there was none of the office pallor. He was, as Eskimo declared, " burnt to a darned cinder."

His hands were red, his lower lip cracked. And he had quit wearing glasses. It seemed to him that they were too indelibly stamped with his former occupation. He squinted badly in the bright sun, but his vision was all right. His ornate cowboy garb was no longer ornate, and to the casual eye he would have appeared about the same as the rest of the range riders.

And, to his great delight, he was picking up a smattering of range lingo, a few well-chosen cuss words, and he could draw his six-shooter out of the holster without shooting it accidentally. He had realised later how close he had been to killing two men, and had promised himself that when he went to town with the boys he would leave his gun at the ranch.

He rode into a well defined cattle-trail and managed to light his cigarette. Since leaving the ranch he had ridden at a walk, but now he spurred his horse into a gallop. It gave him a thrill to ride alone ; to know that critical eyes were not watching his riding ability. The mare was willing to run, but he curbed her slightly. He tried to remember a song that Eskimo sang, but the words escaped him.

In his reckless abandon he stood up in his stirrups, as he had seen Johnny Grant do many times, whipped off his sombrero, and slapped the mare across the rump.

The next thing he realised was that the mare's ears had disappeared with a terrible lurch, and that he was again flying through space. He struck sitting down in the sand, and skidded along for several feet before stopping. He was badly jarred, but unhurt. His sombrero sailed into the brush, and the mare kept right on, going for a hundred feet or so, where she whirled around, cut across a little ridge, and went back toward the AK.

" That was an awful fool thing to do."

The voice seemed to come from nowhere. Jimmy Legg stretched his neck and looked around. Standing in the trail, just a few feet beyond him, was a girl—Marion Taylor. Jimmy Legg shut one eye and considered her gravely. He was sure he was mistaken, and wondered whether this could be a mirage. Oyster had told him of many mirages in that country, but he had never mentioned one of a pretty girl, who could talk.

" What was a fool thing ? " asked Jimmy.

" Slappin' a horse, and gettin' throwed off," she replied.

Jimmy got to his feet, braced his legs, and stared at her.

" I dunno just what did happen," he confessed foolishly.

Marion eyed him gravely, and he thought she was the prettiest girl he had ever seen.

" You must be the new man at the AK," she said.

" Yes, ma'am, I'm the new cowpuncher."

" Cowpuncher ? "

" Well, yea-a-ah." He tried to imitate Johnny Grant.

The girl laughed.

" I'm James Eat—Jimmy Legg," he stammered.

" I am Marion Taylor," she said, smiling. " We own the Double Bar 8."

" Oh, yes."

They considered each other silently for a while. Jimmy glanced around.

" Where's your horse, Miss Taylor ? "

She coloured slightly.

" Got away from me. Spike hates snakes, you see. We found a big rattler, and I got off to shoot it. I didn't want to shoot off Spike, because he hates a gun ; so I got off, and when I shot the rattler, Spike yanked away."

Jimmy nodded.

" We've both lost our horses, it seems. You see, I don't know anything about snakes."

" No ? You know a rattler when you see one, don't you ? "

" No, I'm sure I wouldn't."

" Then you better walk carefully, because we've got plenty of them around here. You'll probably see one on your way back to the AK."

" Possibly," said Jimmy gravely. " But I'm not going back—not now. You see, I'm going to take you home first."

" Oh, no," Marion smiled shortly. " It's only about three miles, you see. I don't mind the walk."

" Well, I'm goin' along," declared Jimmy. " You might get bit by a snake, or—or——"

Marion smiled with amusement.

" Do you think you could protect me from a rattler, Mr. Legg ? "

" I dunno," confessed Jimmy.

He glanced at the Colt, which swung from her hip.

" Can you hit anything with that ? "

" Sometimes. Why ? "

" I was just wondering."

" Can you shoot ? " she asked.

" Yea-a-a-ah, sure," solemnly. Then he laughed outright. " I almost killed the sheriff and a prominent attorney, I believe. It—it went off when I wasn't looking, you see."

" I heard about it."

They both laughed.

" Why not walk to the AK ? " asked Marion. " It's a lot nearer than the Double Bar 8. We— I could get a horse there."

Jimmy shook his head quickly.

" Everybody is away, and the only horse there is one they call Cowcatcher."

" Cowcatcher ! " exclaimed Marion. " I'm sure I don't want to ride him."

" You couldn't, anyway. I rode him to-day, and he ran rather wild, it seems. We knocked the horses from under the sheriff and the deputy, and ran into the corral fence, where Cowcatcher hurt his shoulder."

Marion looked at him in amazement. She knew the reputation of that outlaw bucker.

" Do you mean to say that you rode Cow-catcher ? "

" Yes, ma'am."

" And were you on him when he quit ? "

" Oh, yes," innocently. " He's not very tame, is he ? " Jimmy laughed softly. " It was lots of fun."

" Lots of fun ? " Marion bit her lip and stared at this strange young man, whose language and actions did not brand him as a man of the ranges, and yet who had ridden the worst horse in the Blue Wells country, and thought it lots of fun.

And yet she had seen him thrown clean at the first pitching buck of a galloping horse. She could see that he had been freshly sunburned, and that his clothes were comparatively new.

" I don't understand you," she told him.

Jimmy looked away, his eyes squinted seriously. " Do you always have to understand any one ? " he asked.

" You're not a cowpuncher, Mr. Legg."

Jimmy turned to her, a half-smile on his wide mouth.

" Do I look as raw as all that, Miss Taylor ? I know I'm not a cowboy, but I'm going to be. Johnny Grant says I'll make a good one, if I live to finish my education."

Marion laughed at his naïve confession.

" I didn't know that anybody ever wanted to be a cowboy," she said. " It's just hard work."

Jimmy Legg looked at her, a curious expression in his eyes.

"And romance," he said slowly. "It is a big world out here. The blue nights, the sweet air of the hills in the morning, the midday, when the air fairly hums with the heat ; and then when the shadows of sunset come, and the birds call—isn't it worth learning to be a cowboy, to live here ? "

"Well, when you see things that way, Mr. Legg. I've lived here almost all my life, and I—maybe I'm so used to it."

"Having cowboys thrown off at your feet ? " grinned Jimmy.

Marion flushed slightly.

"No, this is the first time. But you see, you are not a regular cowpuncher."

"I suppose that does make a difference. Perhaps we better start walking, Miss Taylor."

"Well, if you insist. I can let you have a horse to ride back to the AK."

"That will be fine. We should be at your ranch in an hour."

"But we won't," laughed Marion. "Any time you walk three miles an hour through this sand, the State of Arizona will give you a medal for bravery. In about fifteen minutes you'll decide that high-heeled boots were never made for walking."

It did not take Jimmy Legg that long to find it out. His left boot rubbed a blister on his heel, and his right boot creased deeply across his toes, adding several more blisters to his grand total. But he gritted his teeth and said nothing.

"Next time I go riding alone," panted Jimmy, "I'm going to tie the lead rope around my waist.

Then, if my horse throws me off and tries to go
home, he'll have to drag me along."

" You've got silk socks on, haven't you ? "
asked Marion. Jimmy admitted that he had.

" No good," said Marion. " Stylish, but terrible.
Wear woollen socks."

" You make me ashamed," confessed Jimmy.
" You travel along as though it was nothing, while
I'm having an awful time. All I need is a handful
of lead-pencils and I'd be a first-class cripple."

The last mile was exquisite torture, but Jimmy
managed to stumble into the patio of the Double
Bar 8 and sit down on the well-curb.

He took off his boots, while Marion drew a fresh
bucket of water. His feet were so swollen that he
could hardly get the boots off, and his silk socks
were in shreds.

He sat on the edge of the curb and soaked his
feet in the cold water of the trough, while Marion
found him a pair of Buck's socks.

" Do you still think there is romance ? " she
asked, as he grimaced over his blisters. He looked
up at her, forgetting the pain in his feet.

" Yes," he said honestly. " You are the Beautiful
Lady, and I am the Knight of the Blistered Feet."
He laughed softly. " As soon as I can get my boots
on, I shall try and slay a dragon for you."

" It isn't going to be a hard season on dragons,"
smiled the girl. " Unless all signs fail, you are
going to have a hard time getting those boots
on."

There was no one else at the ranch. A

mocking-bird sang from the patio wall, and a huge pepper-tree threw a shade across the two at the well.

" Let's forget about blistered feet," said Jimmy Legg. " Tell me about this country, Miss Taylor. I'm a tenderfoot—and, oh, so tender just now," he laughed ruefully. " But I don't mind. I didn't know there were girls like you in this country. I've read stories of Arizona, where the handsome hero fought forty men, and won the heroine, who was very beautiful. But it doesn't seem true to me, because I haven't seen forty men since I came."

" And there are no beautiful heroines," she said.

" Well," smiled Jimmy, " they didn't have to do any heroic things. They were merely the central figure—some one to do great things for, don't you see."

" I suppose so," smiled the girl. " But forty Arizona men would be rather a handful for one man to whip."

Jimmy nodded seriously.

" Yes, I suppose a man would have to have quite an incentive."

" He might start in on one and work his way up," said a strange voice.

They turned quickly to see Tex Alden, who had come in so softly that they did not hear him. Perhaps they were too engrossed in their own conversation to hear him.

Tex smiled at Marion, but the look he gave Jimmy was anything but friendly.

" Hallo, Tex," said Marion. " We didn't hear you ride up."

" Naturally."

Marion ignored his sarcasm.

" Tex Alden, this is Mr. Legg," she said.

" From the AK," supplemented Jimmy.

" Runnin' a dude ranch out there, are they ? "
Tex did not offer his hand to Jimmy, who did not
offer his.

Marion explained how she had lost her horse,
and how she and Jimmy had met in the hills.
But Tex could not see any humour in the situation.
It was too much of a coincidence to suit him.

" Outside of that," he said dryly, " I've got
some bad news for you, Marion. Your father,
Buck, and Peeler are in jail at Blue Wells."

" In jail ? " Marion stared at Tex. " Why,
what for, Tex ? "

Tex shrugged his shoulders.

" Robbin' that train, it seems."

" But they never robbed that train, Tex ! "

" Quien sabe ? They're in jail. Between the
sheriff and that railroad detective they cooked up
some sort of a case against 'em. I didn't get all
of it, but it seems that Olson, Porter, and the
detective, a man named Wade, came out here to
the ranch. During the conversation the detective
kicked the dog. Buck bawled him out for it, and
the detective asked Buck if it was his dog.

" Buck said it was, it seems. The sheriff asked
Buck how long he had owned the dog, and Buck
said he raised it. They've got the dog in jail, too,
holding him until they can get the engineer, fireman, and the express messenger here to identify

it.   From what I can hear, the dog belonged to the bandits."

Jimmy Legg stared across the patio, his eyes smarting in the bright sunlight.

"Buck never raised that dog," said Marion hoarsely.   "It was a dog that picked up with them—with dad, Buck, and Peeler."

"How long ago?" asked Tex.

"The——" Marion faltered.   "It was the day after the robbery that he came here with them, Tex.   They had been back on Yellow Horn mesa, looking for cattle.   They left the day of the robbery."

"What kind of a dog was it?" asked Jimmy Legg.

"Just a stray mongrel," said Marion.   "It was coarse-haired and sort of a yellowish-red colour."

There was no question in Jimmy's mind that this dog was Geronimo.

"Quite a lot of strays comin' to this country lately," said Tex Alden, as he looked meaningly at Jimmy.

Jimmy caught the implication, but said nothing. He did not want to have any trouble with Tex Alden.

"I suppose yore father can prove that the dog don't belong here, can't he?" asked Tex.

"I don't see why not," replied Marion quickly.

"I was just wonderin', Marion.   There's so many dogs around here that nobody pays much attention to 'em.   Anyway, the sheriff says that even if they can prove away the dog, they'll have to show him where they were the night of the robbery."

" But they can't—except their word, Tex. They were back on Yellow Horn mesa, and no one saw them back there."

Tex smiled.

" Makes it kinda tough. If yo're aimin' to ride to Blue Wells, I'll ride back with yuh."

Marion looked at Jimmy, who was sitting on the edge of the curb, his sore feet encased in a pair of Buck's woollen socks.

" I suppose I'll have to go," she said slowly. " But I don't like to leave the ranch alone. If Mr. Legg will stay here until I get back——"

" That won't hardly do," said Tex quickly. " You don't know this man, Marion. We can get some one in Blue Wells——"

" Oh, I don't mind staying," said Jimmy earnestly.

" But you can't stay here with a strange man."

" I meant—until I got back," said Marion coldly. " And how long since you started running the Double Bar 8, Tex Alden ? "

Tex flushed hotly.

" I'm not tryin' to run the ranch, Marion."

" Then don't. I think Spike is around by the corral ; so if you will excuse me, I'll get him."

Tex made no effort to get the horse for her, because he wanted a word in private with Jimmy Legg. After she had gone out through the patio gate, Tex turned to Jimmy.

" Let me give you a word of advice, young feller.

Yo're new to this country; so jist take my word for it that we don't want strangers around. You tramped in here; now tramp out. The climate of the Blue Wells country is sure damp for yore kind."

"I don't think I understand what you mean," said Jimmy. "I'm not a tramp, Mr. Alden."

"You walked into Blue Wells. Anyway, you told the sheriff yuh did. Ain't that trampin'?"

Jimmy smiled and shook his head.

"There's a difference, I think, between a man who merely walks in, and a man who tramps in."

"Not a bit of difference around here, Legg. I'll probably ride back with Miss Taylor; and I don't want to find you here. If yo're wise, you'll heed what I'm tellin' yuh. I've give yuh a fair warnin'."

"Reminds me of what Miss Taylor said about rattlesnakes," said Jimmy innocently. "They nearly always buzz before they strike, it seems. She says that is what makes them less to be feared than any other poisonous snakes."

Tex stepped in closer to Jimmy, his eyes snapping.

"Do you mean to call me a snake?"

"No; only the warning. And don't forget, you called me a tramp."

"If you wasn't such an ignorant —— fool," began Tex—but at that moment Marion made her appearance, leading the blue-black horse which had left her stranded in the hills, and Tex turned to her, leaving his statement to Jimmy unfinished.

"Mr. Legg won't be able to stay," stated Tex. "If you'll show him which horse to ride back to the AK, Marion——"

" I've changed my mind," said Jimmy, hugging his knees. " I'm going to stay, Miss Taylor."

" Thank you, Mr. Legg."

Marion turned away to hide a smile. She realised that Tex had tried to make Jimmy's decision for him, and she was glad that Jimmy defied him.

Tex glared at Jimmy, but said nothing. Marion waved at Jimmy from the patio gate, but Tex did not turn his head. Marion had little to say to Tex on the way to Blue Wells. He tried to apologise to her for what he had said to Jimmy Legg, but she paid little attention to his excuses. As a result, Tex rode to Blue Wells with a distinct peeve against this stranger.

He left Marion at the doorway of the sheriff's office, and met Lee Barnhardt a little farther up the street. The lawyer might have ignored Tex's presence had not Tex stepped in beside him. It was the first time they had met since the day after the hold-up.

" What do yuh know about the arrest of Taylor, Buck, and the half-breed ? " asked Tex. Barnhardt glanced sideways at Tex, and a knowing smile twisted his lips.

" I know it's probably lucky for some folks, Tex. You see, I've talked with them, and I'll probably defend their case ; so I haven't any information to give out."

" Yea-a-ah ? "

" Yea-a-ah." Barnhardt mimicked Tex's drawl perfectly, but the expression in Tex's eyes caused

Barnhardt's Adam's-apple to jerk convulsively. The lawyer was a physical coward, and Tex knew it ; so he grasped Barnhardt by the sleeve, whirled him around, and slammed his back against the front of the office.

"—— you ! " gritted Tex. " I've stood about all I'm goin' to stand from you, Lee. Yo're as crooked as a snake in a cactus patch, and we both know it. You told me about that Santa Rita pay-roll, because you wanted yore share. Now, —— yuh—get it, if yuh can ! "

Tex stepped back, his eyes narrowed dangerously, as he looked at Barnhardt's thin face, which twisted to a sneering grin, when he felt sure that Tex was not going to do him bodily harm.

" All right, Tex," he said hoarsely. " No bad feelings, I hope."

Tex shook his head slowly.

" I don't *sabe* you, Lee," he said softly. " Mebbe some day I'm goin' to have to kill you."

Tex spoke in a matter-of-fact way, as though the killing of Lee Barnhardt would be merely a disagreeable task. Barnhardt smiled crookedly.

" You don't need to threaten me, Tex," he said.

" Oh, that's not a threat."

Barnhardt straightened his collar.

" You called me a crook," he remarked. " You can't prove anything, Tex ; but you embezzled eight thousand dollars—and I can prove it."

" How can yuh ? You haven't the bill of sale, nor a copy of it. You had nothing to do with the sale. The cheque was made out to me."

" All right," Barnhardt laughed shortly. " In two weeks the Fall round-up will be held, Tex. There's going to be a shortage of X Bar 6 stock to account for. My report will show this, and I'll have to explain just what happened—unless——"

" Unless what ? "

" Unless you shoot square with me, Tex."

" In other words," said Tex coldly, " if I'll play a crooked game with you, you'll protect me, eh ? "

" You don't need to be so virtuous ! " snapped Barnhardt. " You're in pretty deep already. And any time I want to, I can cut you loose from your present job. Don't forget that I can do you a lot of harm, if I want to, Tex. One of these days that X Bar 6 is going to be mine."

" Yea-a-ah ? How do yuh figure that, Lee ? "

" That's my business. You think things over, Tex."

Tex nodded shortly.

" All right. What kind of a case have they got against Taylor ? "

" I don't know. That Wade, the railroad detective, seems to think the dog links 'em pretty close to the case, but he's got to wait until the engine crew and the messenger identify the dog as being the one that was on the express car."

" Marion says it's a dog that picked up with them the day after the hold-up. I don't remember any such a dog around the Double Bar 8."

" Well, you don't need to worry about it, do you ? "

" Why not ? I expect to marry Taylor's daughter."

" Well ? She's not under arrest. You better look out for Le Moyne, Tex. He's got the same ideas that you have, and I understand that Apostle Paul thinks a lot of Le Moyne."

" Le Moyne doesn't interest me, Lee."

" Sure he don't. But he don't have to interest you. Le Moyne is a handsome devil, and if I was in your boots——"

" Well, you're not ! " Tex flushed angrily. " I've got to help Marion find some woman to stay at the ranch with her. She can't stay there alone. That tenderfoot from the AK was there when I left. His horse pitched him off in the hills, and he wore his feet out walkin' to the Double Bar 8."

" His name is Legg, isn't it ? " queried Barnhardt.

" Yeah."

" What else do you know about him, Tex ? "

" Not a thing—do you ? "

" Only what Johnny Grant said. Legg told him that he used to be a book-keeper in San Francisco."

" Yeah ? Well, he better go back and sling some more ink."

Barnhardt smiled slowly.

" And he's staying at the Double Bar 8, is he ? "

" Not very long, he ain't ! " snapped Tex.

He whirled on his heel and looked down toward the sheriff's office, where Marion was just coming out, accompanied by the sheriff.

" How long before they can identify that dog, Lee ? " he asked.

" When the train gets in to-night, Tex."

" Uh-huh. I'll see yuh later, Lee."

" All right ; and in the meantime you better think over some of the things I've told you."

But Tex did not reply. Marion had mounted her horse. Tex called to her, but she did not reply, as she spurred her horse to a gallop, heading toward home. Tex swore softly and went on, joining the sheriff at the doorway of the office.

" Hyah, Tex," greeted the sheriff.

" All right, Scotty," grunted Tex. " Mind lettin' me see the Taylor family ? "

The sheriff shook his head.

" Can't do it, Tex. I've got my orders from the prosecutor. After t'night, yuh maybe can ; but no chance, until after we know a little more about things."

Tex scowled heavily.

" What evidence have yuh got, Scotty ? "

" Dog. Answers the description."

" Yea-a-ah ? "

Tex leaned one shoulder against the wall of the building and began rolling a cigarette. He looked quizzically at the sheriff as he said :—

" Scotty, did yuh ever wonder why them three men locked yuh in yore own jail ? "

The sheriff considered the question gravely, as if it had never occurred to him before. He smiled softly and shook his head.

" No ; did you, Tex ? "

" It's none of my business, Scotty."

" No ? You don't think Eskimo, Johnny, and Oyster had anythin' to do with the hold-up, do yuh ? "

"I didn't say they did, Scotty."

"There was four men in that hold-up. Old George Bonnette was in Blue Wells that night. They'd 'a' had to get an outsider to help 'em, Tex. We've got to find four men."

"But there's only three in yore jail right now, Scotty."

"Yeah; there's still the owner of the dog."

"Then yuh don't think the dog belongs to Taylor?"

"No, I don't. The man who owns the dog is the man who got on the express car at Encinas, and fought with the messenger. The dog was just a blind for that man to get on there. He was the fourth one of the gang, and he probably didn't figure on the messenger puttin' up a fight. He caught up with the express car as quick as possible and took the dog. The fact that he took a chance to get the dog makes it look like a cinch that if we can find the owner of that dog, we can land the whole bunch."

It was a long explanation for Scotty Olson, and he was all out of breath.

"How about that feller Legg at the AK, Scotty? He'd make a fourth man."

"Him!" Scotty laughed. "Which man would he make? Not the big feller that fought the messenger. And —— knows he ain't one of the masked men that blew the safe."

"Don't be too sure. He'd look pretty big behind a black mask, looking over the top of a six-gun. That engine crew was so scared they wouldn't have known whether they were big men or small ones."

" How do you know how scared they was, Tex ?

The sheriff snapped the question quickly. Tex stiffened slightly, and his shoulder swayed away from the wall.

" Just figurin' 'em to be human," he said softly.

" Oh, yeah." The sheriff's smile was hidden behind his big moustache. " I reckon we'll get along all right. It takes time to figure out things, Tex. Wade's no fool. He's investigatin' every clue—him and Porter. I understand that the Santa Rita has hired a detective. Him and Le Moyne are on the case, kinda workin' independent of my office, I suppose." Scotty smiled. " But that's all right. We want the men who got that thirty thousand."

Tex nodded coldly.

" Good luck to yuh, Scotty. But if I was you, I wouldn't look for them men in Blue Wells. They're a long way from here, I'll betcha."

" I'm no palmist," said Scotty slowly. " If they're out of the county I can't do nothin', but if they're around here, I'm goin' after 'em good and hard."

" Sure," nodded Tex, and went after his horse, while the sheriff looked after him quizzically.

" I wonder what you know, Tex Alden," he said to himself. " I seen yuh talkin' with Lee Barnhardt—and he'll prob'ly defend Taylor, if this comes to court. By golly, I'm gettin' suspicious of everybody. Wade says you've got to suspect everybody, if yo're goin' to be a successful detective ; so I expect I'm startin' out in the right way."

CHAPTER VIII

A REGULAR JOB

IT was supper time at the AK ranch when Jimmy Legg rode in. The boys had discovered his horse when they returned, and had decided that Jimmy had been thrown. They were going to wait until after supper before starting a search.

He told them of the incident and of the long walk to the Double Bar 8 ranch.

" Didja leave that girl alone there ? " asked Eskimo.

" She went back to town," explained Jimmy. " I guess she wanted to be there when the railroad men tried to identify that dog, and she said she'd stay in Blue Wells all night."

" I'd kinda like to be there too," said Johnny Grant. " I've been at the Taylor ranch quite a lot, but I don't remember any dog of that description."

" Let's all go in after supper," suggested Oyster. " I've got a few dollars that's restless."

Old George Bonnette called Jimmy aside after supper.

" What do yuh aim to do ? " asked the old man. Jimmy smiled foolishly.

" I kinda wanted to be a cowpuncher," he confessed, lapsing into the dialect easily.

"Yuh do, eh?" Bonnette smiled. "That's quite an ambition, don'tcha think? Forty a month, and feed. Yo're educated, Legg. I don't *sabe* why yuh want to be a puncher."

"I've got a reason, Mr. Bonnette."

"Some girl dare yuh to be a cowboy?"

"There's a woman in the case," confessed Jimmy.

Bonnette grunted softly and helped himself to a liberal chew of tobacco.

"I thought as much," he grinned. "Well, you ain't—yet. I'm full up on hired hands right now, Legg. It'll soon be round-up time, and yuh might come in handy.

"It'll mean a lot of hard work. I can't pay yuh a cowpuncher's wages, because yuh don't *sabe* the work well enough to earn it; but I'll pay yuh half salary. It'll sure be an education to you, if yuh want to be a puncher. But I'm —— if I know why yuh want to."

"Thanks," smiled Jimmy. "Johnny Grant asked you to do this, didn't he?"

"Well, he said yuh was jist brainless enough to make a good puncher, if that's what yuh mean."

"Don't cowpunchers have any brains, Mr. Bonnette?"

"Huh!" The old man spat explosively. "Evidence is all agin' 'em! If they had any brains, they wouldn't punch cows."

Jimmy thanked him for the half-pay job, and rode away with the three cowpunchers, after Bonnette had warned them not to antagonise the sheriff again.

" Yo're gettin' a bad reputation," declared Bonnette. " Next thing I know I'll have some cripples hobblin' around here."

" We're plumb antiseptic now," assured Johnny Grant. " There ain't money enough in the crowd to start anythin'."

They headed for town, talking about the robbery. None of them had told Jimmy about their battle with the engineer and fireman. The AK boys were tight-mouthed over it, because they didn't want to be hauled in on the case, and they were just a little suspicious about Jimmy Legg.

Near where the AK road paralleled the railroad it intersected with the road from Encinas, and as they neared the intersection they saw two riders coming from the east, jogging along through the dust, as if time was of no importance.

The four riders from the AK drew rein and waited for the two cowboys, thinking them to be two of the Blue Wells riders. But in this they were mistaken, as the two riders were strangers to the country.

One of them was a lean, rangy sort of individual, with a long face, prominent nose, wide mouth, and widely-spaced blue eyes, set in a mass of tiny wrinkles. The other rider was of medium height, rather blocky of countenance, wide-mouthed, and with deep grin-wrinkles, which seemed to end beneath a firm jaw. His eyes were wide, blue, and innocent.

Both men were dressed in range costume, well-worn, weathered. Their riding rigs were polished from much usage, and the boys from the AK noted that their belts and holsters were hand-made by men who knew the sag of human anatomy. The tall man removed his battered sombrero, disclosing a crop of roan-coloured hair, and the wide grin, which suffused his whole face, showed a set of strong, white teeth.

" Howdy," smiled the tall man. " Is this the road to Blue Wells ? "

" It sure is," grinned Johnny. He instinctively liked this tall man, whose grin was contagious.

" Well, that's good," nodded the shorter man.

Johnny Grant's eyes had strayed to their two horses, which were branded on the left shoulder with a Circle X, the iron of a ranch about twelve miles east of Encinas.

" We're goin' to Blue Wells," said Eskimo, " and we'll see that yuh don't stray."

" That's sure kind of yuh," said the innocent-eyed one. " You don't know what a load that takes off my mind."

Eskimo squinted closely at him, but could not determine whether the man was joking or not. Johnny Grant moved his horse in closer.

" My name's Grant," he told them.

He turned in his saddle and introduced the others, concluding with Jimmy Legg, of whom he said :—

" This is Jimmy Legg. He wants to be a cow-puncher so badly that he don't know what to do— and we're teachin' him."

" I'm sure he'll make a good one," said the innocent-eyed stranger, sizing up the uncomfortable

Jimmy. "Yuh can't hardly tell him from one now. If yuh hadn't told us about him, we'd never know but what he was a top-hand. My name is Stevens. My pardner answers to the name of Hartley, and we're proud to know you gents."

"Proud to know you," nodded the boys of the AK.

"We might as well mosey along," said Johnny. "You aimin' to stay in Blue Wells a while, gents?"

"All depends," said "Hashknife" Hartley. "We hear that the Fall round-up is about to start, and thought we might hook on with some cow oufit. We ain't never been in here, yuh see."

"Well, yuh might," admitted Johnny. "I dunno how the rest of the ranches are fixed for help."

"Does anythin' ever happen around here?" asked "Sleepy" Stevens. "You know what I mean—any excitement?"

"Everythin' happens," said Eskimo, and they proceeded to regale them with a story of the robbery.

Johnny Grant went into details regarding the dog, which figured in the evidence, and by the time they got to Blue Wells, Hashknife and Sleepy knew practically all the details, as far as was known.

"We'll know more about it when the train gets in," said Oyster. "Them trainmen say they can identify the dog, if it's the same one."

They rode in to Blue Wells, and tied their horses at the Oasis hitch-rack. Hashknife and Sleepy went to the Oasis hotel, where they secured a room, after which they took their horses to the livery-stable.

Quite a crowd of people had gathered in Blue Wells, waiting for the train to come in. There was much speculation as to whether or not the trainmen could identify the dog as being the one on the express car. Tex Alden was in town, as was Le Moyne. Johnny Grant pointed out Le Moyne, and introduced Hashknife to Tex.

Hashknife did not strike Tex for a job, but merely exchanged a few words with him. They met the sheriff in the Oasis, and Johnny introduced him to Hashknife. But the sheriff was not friendly, and Johnny explained the reasons why. They found Al Porter and Wade, the railroad detective, but Porter gave Johnny a wide berth. He could see that Johnny had imbibed a few drinks, and Mr. Porter did not want his dignity disturbed.

The train arrived on time, and the crowd repaired to the hall over Abe Moon's store, which was used as a court-room. Jimmy Legg had imbibed a large drink of liquor, which had caused him to forget certain things, and as a result he found himself in the hall, almost rubbing shoulders with the express messenger.

The sheriff ordered every one to sit down and not to interfere with the proceedings. He brought Apostle Paul Taylor, Buck Taylor, and Peeler into the room and seated them against the wall. The half-breed was frightened, but the Taylor family were cool. Marion was there, and joined her father. Hashknife and Sleepy remained in the background, watching the proceedings.

Al Porter, the deputy, brought the dog into

the room, a short piece of rope tied to its collar. It was Geronimo! Jimmy Legg gasped, drew his hat farther over his face, and acted indifferent.

Geronimo apparently thought that the gathering was for his special benefit, for he cavorted on the end of the rope, barking, whining, sniffing. Suddenly he whirled around, headed toward Jimmy Legg, head up, sniffing. The scent of the man who had befriended him!

His sudden lunge almost yanked the rope out of Porter's hands, and his paws scraped across Jimmy Legg's knees, when the angry deputy jerked the dog back to him. Jimmy gasped with relief, looked up from under the low-pulled brim of his hat, and found the railroad detective looking at him.

The engineer and fireman positively identified the dog. The express messenger was not so positive, but said that it surely looked like the same dog. Johnny Grant, with a few drinks of liquor under his belt, walked out and took a close look at the dog.

" I've been at the Double Bar 8 a lot of times," he told the sheriff, " but I never seen that dog before. I like dogs, Scotty. I never miss a chance to play with a dog, and if that dog was a reg'lar at the Double Bar 8, I'd shore know it."

" Buck swears he raised it from a pup," replied the sheriff.

" Buck wasn't telling the truth," said Marion. " He was mad at you for kicking it, and questioning the ownership."

" When did you see it the first time, Miss Taylor ? " asked the sheriff.

" When it came home with dad, Buck, and Peeler."

" The day after the hold-up, eh ? "

" Yes."

The railroad detective sauntered up.

" Where did they say they got the dog, Miss Taylor ? " he asked.

" Why, they said it picked up with them, when they were on their way home from Yellow Horn mesa."

The sheriff smiled and told Porter to take the dog back to the office.

" I reckon we'll hang on to the dog until we find out who owns it," he said.

" But you can't hold us any longer," protested Apostle Paul.

" Can't I ? "

" It's a bailable offence," said the detective. " I suppose you'll have a hearing to-morrow, and have your bail set."

" And have to stay in jail to-night, eh ? "

" Yes ; unless the judge wants to hold a night session."

" Which he won't," declared Porter. " Old Judge Parkridge will take his own sweet time—and it won't be at night."

The sheriff removed his prisoners and the crowd filed down the stairs. Jimmy Legg moved in beside Marion and went down to the street with her. Most of the crowd headed for the Oasis, and Tex Alden was with them. He stopped long enough to see that Jimmy Legg was with Marion, but went on.

"Gee, that's a dirty shame, Miss Taylor," said Jimmy. "They haven't anything on your father, nor any of the rest."

"Oh, I know it, Mr. Legg ; but what can we do ? "

"You might start in by calling me Jimmy. I hate the rest of my name. It's James Eaton Legg. Sounds like a cannibal, doesn't it. Parents never stop to think, when they're naming innocent children."

"All right, Jimmy—if you'll call me Marion. Every one does. We are not formal out here in the wilderness."

"I'm glad you're not. My feet feel fine in those socks. I'll buy me some to-night and give Buck a new pair."

"Don't bother about that, Jimmy."

"No bother at all. Say, that Tex Alden don't like me, does he ? "

"Possibly not."

"Does he—— ? " Jimmy hesitated.

"Does he what, Jimmy ? "

"Oh, that's a little too personal, Marion."

"I suppose so. You meant to ask me if Tex thought he had the right to say who I shall speak to, didn't you ? "

"Well, has he ? "

"Only in his own mind."

Jimmy laughed softly.

"Some folks are blessed with wonderful imaginations. Are you going to stay at the hotel to-night ? "

"Yes, I'll stay there to-night, anyway."

They walked up the street and met Chet Le Moyne in front of Abe Moon's store. He shook hands with Marion, who introduced him to Jimmy.

"You are paymaster of the Santa Rita mine, aren't you?" asked Jimmy. "I thought that's what Johnny Grant said."

"Yes," said Le Moyne patronisingly. "And you are the new cowboy at the AK ranch."

"Yea-a-ah," drawled Jimmy. "That's me."

Marion laughed.

"He's going to be a good one, too."

"As good as any," laughed Jimmy.

"You've had a good start, I hear," chuckled Le Moyne. "They tell me that you almost killed Scotty Olson and Lee Barnhardt the day you came here."

"And never got arrested," laughed Jimmy. "This is a wonderful country."

Hashknife Hartley and Sleepy Stevens came out of the store, halted on the edge of the sidewalk to light their cigarettes, and went on across the street.

"Who are those men?" asked Marion. "I noticed the tall one looking at me in the court-room."

"One—the tall one—is named Hartley," said Jimmy. "The other is Stevens. They met us at the forks of the road this evening, and rode in with us. They're strangers here, it seems."

Marion and Jimmy strolled on toward the hotel, and Le Moyne went to the store. Hashknife and Sleepy mingled with the crowd in the Oasis, and finally took seats at a table near the rear of the place. Business was good, all the games filled, and the bar was doing a big business.

The engineer, fireman, and the express messenger came over to the saloon and joined the crowd at the bar.

" Plenty of excitement," observed Hashknife. " This hold-up seems to have kinda stirred up Blue Wells, Sleepy."

" Yeah." Sleepy did not seem to be very enthusiastic.

" Aw, shake yore hide," grinned Hashknife. " You act like a mourner at a funeral, cowboy."

" I'm all right," muttered Sleepy. " But it makes me tired. Every time we go anywhere, somethin' happens. There's no peace anywhere. When them fellers was tellin' about that hold-up, yore nose was twitchin' like the nose of a pointer dog. Dang it, me and you didn't come here to hunt bandits."

Hashknife chuckled softly.

" And I'm not huntin' 'em, Sleepy. What do yuh think of that ? I ain't lost no bandits. It's nothin' to me how many pay-rolls they steal."

" Then don't say nothin' more about that girl, Hashknife. Ever since you got a look at her, you've spoke about her several times."

" Pshaw ! I didn't realise it, Sleepy. Mebbe I just remarked about her folks all bein' in jail."

" Let 'em stay in jail," grunted Sleepy heartlessly. " They prob'ly robbed that train. We didn't come here to——"

" I know that sentence by heart, Sleepy. And you ought to know my reply. But that don't alter the fact that she's one pretty girl."

" There yuh go ! " gloomily.

Johnny Grant had spotted them and was coming their way, slightly unsteady on his legs, but grinning widely.

" C'mon and have a drink," he urged. " I jist runs four-bits into a ten-spot in the black-jack game. If yuh don't drink yuh can have a see-gar. But I warns yuh, their see-gars are a lot older than the liquor they sell. C'mon up to the bar and meet some of the folks."

Neither of them wanted a drink, but they did want to be friendly with Johnny Grant and his crowd ; so they elbowed their way to the bar. Ed Gast and Bill Bailey of the X Bar 6 were at the bar, and Johnny introduced them, after which he deposited his money on the bar, and demanded action.

" Beatin' that game is as easy as holdin' up a train," he declared, chuckling. " Runs four-bits up to ten dollars, and sticks my thumb at m' nose at the dealer."

Hashknife noticed that the sheriff was at the bar, and that Johnny's remark interested him.

" Except that yuh can't very well lose at holdin' up a train," added Eskimo Swensen, who had caught the sheriff's reflection in the mirror. " If yuh ever get the money in yore hands, yo're as safe as a church. Political affluence shore don't make a sheriff a man-catcher."

Realising that this conversation was for his

benefit, the sheriff moved away from the bar, while the AK boys chuckled over their drinks. Even Sleepy Stevens shed his pessimistic attitude and grinned.

"These are home folks," he said to Hashknife. "It appears that the sheriff ain't standin' very well with the AK."

"Aw, he's all right," said Oyster. "Scotty's as good as the average sheriff, except that he's too serious. He'd give his right eye for a chance to prove first degree murder ag'in the whole AK outfit, because we devil him. He's——"

The men at the bar jerked around when from out in the street came the unmistakable sound of a revolver shot.

"Somebody celebratin'," decided Johnny Grant, as the sheriff and several men moved to the doorway and went outside.

They gulped their drinks, and went out into the street, where the only lights were those from the saloon and store windows.

"Somebody tryin' to be funny," grumbled the sheriff.

He went back into the Oasis. Some men had come from Moon's store across the street, evidently wondering who had fired the shot. Two men with a lantern were fussing around a wagon in front of the blacksmith shop. One of the men came across from the store and went into the Oasis. It was Chet Le Moyne.

"Well, I reckon it was some puncher wishful of makin' a noise," decided Johnny Grant.

They turned and were going back into the saloon, when some one called from the hotel, which was across the street, and about a block north of the Oasis.

" C'mere ! " yelled the man. He was evidently calling to some one in the hotel. " Come out and help me with this feller ! "

" That sounds like somethin' wrong," said Hashknife. " Let's go and see what it is."

They hurried up the street and crossed to the hotel, where several men had gathered around a man who was lying flat on the ground.

" He's been shot," they heard one of them say. " Better pack him into the hotel and send for a doctor."

A man scratched a match, but it flickered out. Hashknife shoved him aside, dropped on his knees beside the man, and ignited a match with a snap of his thumb-nail. The illumination showed a gory face, gray as ashes, where the blood had not stained.

" My —— ! " blurted Johnny. " It's Jimmy Legg ! "

He dropped on his knees beside Hashknife, grasping Jimmy's shoulders.

" Hey ! Jimmy ! " he exclaimed.

" Don't shake him ! " roared Eskimo. " You big idiot ! "

" Somebody go and find a doctor," ordered Hashknife. " We'll take him in the hotel."

They carried him into the little hotel office, where there was light enough for them to discover that Jimmy Legg had missed death by a very scant margin. The bullet had struck him just above his left ear, slanted along his skull, and had furrowed deeply for about three inches.

Some one had gone after a doctor, and in the meantime Hashknife secured a basin of water and a towel, with which he mopped some of the blood away.

"I heard that shot," said the proprietor of the hotel. "I thought it was somebody just makin' a noise. Say, I seen that young feller talkin' to Miss Taylor not five minutes ago. They was just outside the door there."

"To Miss Taylor, eh?" Johnny blinked at the lamp. "Is she here now?"

The commotion in the office attracted Marion's attention, and she was standing in the hallway door when Johnny spoke.

"I'm here," she said. "What do you want of me?"

The cowboys removed their hats, as Johnny went toward her.

"You was talkin' with Jimmy Legg a few minutes ago?" he asked.

"Why, yes." She was unable to see the man on the floor.

"Well, he got shot," said Johnny bluntly.

"Shot?" Marion jerked forward. "Did somebody—not dead?"

"He ain't badly hurt, ma'am," said Hashknife. "The doctor will fix him up in no time."

Marion came forward to where she could see. Her face was white and her two hands were clenched tightly, as she looked at Jimmy Legg, stretched on the floor.

" Why, I just left him a minute or so ago," she whispered. " Where did it happen ? "

" Jist out in the street," replied Johnny. " I want to find the jasper that shot the poor devil ! "

" If yuh do, don't keep it to yourself," growled Eskimo.

Marion stopped at the desk, bracing herself with one hand.

" Who would shoot him ? " wondered Eskimo. " He wouldn't hurt anybody. If it had been one of us——"

" That would be justified," finished Johnny Grant.

Jimmy Legg lifted his head and stared around, blinking his eyes.

" What was it ? " he whispered.

" Somebody took a shot at yuh," said Johnny quickly.

Jimmy Legg felt of his head.

" Hit me, didn't they ? "

At this moment the doctor arrived, ordered them to carry Jimmy to a room, and proceeded to fix up the wound. Marion insisted on helping him, and Jimmy blinked his gratitude.

" Did you see the man who shot at you ? " asked Marion.

" I never knew I was shot, until I woke up, Marion. You had just gone into the hotel, and I started to cross the street, when I saw a big flash, like an explosion. But I never heard the noise."

The doctor washed and sewed up the wound. It was a painful proceeding, but Jimmy gritted his teeth and did not make a sound.

"You better get a room here at the hotel and go to bed," advised the doctor. But Jimmy refused.

"I'm all right," he insisted. "It aches a little, but not enough to put me in bed. Gee, it sure knocked me out!"

"And you're lucky to be alive," said the doctor, packing his kit-bag. "An inch farther to the right, and you'd have no top on your head right now."

The crowd was just outside the door, waiting for the doctor to finish, and they crowded in, hardly giving the doctor a chance to wriggle his way out into the hall. Jimmy held out his hand to Marion, disregarding the clamouring cowboys.

"Thank you," he said. "It was nice of you to stay with me."

Marion coloured slightly, and her reply was drowned in Johnny Grant's greeting.

"Hyah, Topknot! Howsa head, Jimmy?"

"Don't jiggle me!" laughed Jimmy. "My face is so tight I can hardly laugh."

"Don't laugh," advised Eskimo. "Now, who do yuh know that might hate yuh enough to shoot yuh, Jimmy?"

Jimmy frowned painfully at the floor, and when he looked up he caught Marion's eye. Tex Alden's threat came back to him :—

"The Blue Wells country is sure damp for your kind."

Jimmy tried to smile, but it was only a grimace.

" I dunno," he said slowly. " I haven't had any trouble with any one here, except that day I accidentally shot at the sheriff and the lawyer."

" But that was an accident," said Johnny. " Nobody blames yuh for that. Somebody wanted to kill yuh, kid."

" Maybe," faltered Jimmy, " they mistook me for somebody else."

As Jimmy spoke he was looking at Marion, and he switched his eyes to Hashknife, who was watching him closely. The eyes of the tall cowboy seemed to bore into him, and Jimmy turned away.

" You was talkin' with Miss Taylor just a minute or so before yuh got shot, eh ? " Oyster Shell had an idea.

" Yes."

" Uh-hah ! "

" What's that got to do with it ? " demanded Johnny.

" Aw, let's go and get a drink," suggested Oyster. " Jimmy is all right. How about yuh, Jimmy ? "

" I'm fine," replied Jimmy. " Except that my feet don't track and there's a ton of rocks on my head—I'm as good as ever."

They moved out of the hotel and headed for the Oasis, where Jimmy was the centre of attraction. Le Moyne and Dug Haley were there. Johnny introduced them to Hashknife and Sleepy, and they all drank to the poor aim of some bushwhacker.

After a few more drinks the AK boys decided to go home. Jimmy's head was bothering him, and Johnny Grant decided that a bunk was the best place for Jimmy Legg. Before they left, the sheriff and deputy bustled in, having just heard of the shooting and wanted a detailed account of it.

" Aw, whatsa use ? " wailed Eskimo. " Somebody popped Jimmy on the head with a bullet, and that's all there is to it. Unless petrification sets in, he'll be able to fall off a horse ag'in to-morrow—as usual. C'mon."

And the sheriff was obliged to get his information from those who knew as much about it as the AK boys did. He went back to his office with Al Porter, and they sat down to discuss it.

" Well, who do yuh think tried to kill the tenderfoot ? " queried Porter.

" If we didn't have three men in jail, facin' a charge of holdin' up a train, I'd say that this here Legg person was the fourth one of the gang, and that some of 'em tried to bump him off for somethin'."

" Well, I'll be —— ! " snorted Porter. " If we can't hang it on to the Taylor gang, that might be worth workin' on, Scotty. But who are these two strange cowpunchers who rode in with the AK gang to-night ? Johnny Grant acts kinda friendly with 'em."

" I don't know, Al. I reckon I'll hit the hay. To-morrow we hold a hearin' for the Taylor gang, and we'll see what we'll see. You better feed that dog before yuh go to bed, or he might mistake old Judge Parkridge for a strip of jerky. He looks like one."

CHAPTER IX

COMPLICATIONS

THE Taylor hearing was more or less of a farce, but it left Apostle Paul, Buck, and Peeler, the half-breed, high and dry in the Blue Wells jail until the next term of court. Old Judge Parkridge, near-sighted, more than slightly deaf, a mummified old jurist, set their bail at one thousand dollars cash, each—bail which no one would furnish.

There was no evidence against them, except the fact that they had the dog, and that they could not prove that they had spent the night on Yellow Horn mesa. So they were formally charged with train robbery and held until the next session of court, which would not be held for three weeks.

Apostle Paul Taylor cursed the judge, who could not hear it, and went back to the jail, followed by Buck and Peeler. Marion was broken-hearted, but did not show it. She sat down in the sheriff's office and tried to reason out just what to do. The Double Bar 8 could not afford to hire men, and she could not do the work alone.

The sheriff did not try to solace her. He was tongue-tied in her presence. Then Tex Alden showed up. He had not been at the hearing, but had been told all about it.

"That's sure tough, Marion," he told her. "I'll tell yuh what I'll do—I'll send some of my men down to run the ranch for yuh, and it won't cost yuh a cent."

"No, thank you, Mr. Alden."

Tex coloured quickly. It was the first time she had ever called him "Mr. Alden."

"Why, what's the matter?" he asked quickly. "What have I done?"

"You know what you did," she retorted. "Please don't bother yourself about my affairs."

Tex stared at her wonderingly.

"Well, for gosh sake!" he blurted. "Hm-m-m-m! Whatsa matter now?"

But Marion turned away from him and stared out through one of the dirty windows. Tex whistled softly and walked outside. He stopped, turned, as if to go back, but changed his mind and went on up the street, whistling unmusically between his teeth, his brow furrowed.

Lee Barnhardt, the lawyer, was coming from his office, and met Tex in front of the general store.

"Wasn't that a verdict, Tex?" he asked.

"Verdict? Oh, yeah." Tex looked thoughtfully at the lean-faced attorney. "I'm wonderin' who'll run the Double Bar 8 until after the trial, Lee?"

"I don't know; never thought about it, Tex. Say, did you hear about that AK tenderfoot getting shot last night?"

"Legg?"

"Yes. Some one shot him last night, almost in front of the hotel."

" Yea-a-ah ? Kill him ? "

" No," Barnhardt laughed. " Skull was too hard, I guess. He had been standing there, talking with Marion Taylor, and just after she went into the hotel, some one shot him. But he was able to ride back to the AK ; so I guess he's all right."

Tex took a deep breath, and looked back toward the sheriff's office. Marion was coming up the street. He turned to Barnhardt.

" I hadn't heard about it, Lee. I left just after the trainmen had identified the dog."

Tex turned on his heel and went across the street, disappearing in the Oasis saloon.

Marion joined Barnhardt and they walked to his office. The girl did not like Barnhardt, but her father had engaged him to handle their defence. Hashknife and Sleepy had talked with several of the cowboys, and it was their opinion that none of the cattle outfits would put on extra men until the round-up.

Hashknife went to the sheriff's office and had a talk with Scotty Olson. Hashknife had heard the cowboys talking about the Double Bar 8, and the fact that there was no one, except the girl to run the ranch. Hashknife explained to the sheriff that he and Sleepy would be willing to run the Double Bar 8, at least until the round-up started, and without wages.

" What's the idea ? " queried Scotty. It looked fishy to him.

" Merely helpin' out," smiled Hashknife. " It'll save us a hotel bill, and we might as well be workin' as settin' around a saloon."

Scotty smoothed his moustache and admitted that it would be a great help to the Taylor family.

" C'mon in and meet Apostle Paul," suggested the sheriff.

Hashknife followed him to the cells and was introduced to Marion's father, who scrutinised Hashknife closely, when the sheriff explained what Hartley and his partner were willing to do.

" I thought mebbe Tex Alden would help us out," said the old man.

" Yuh can hang that idea up in the smoke-house," said the sheriff. " Tex met yore daughter a while ago, and she kinda snubbed him up real short, Paul."

"Yea-a-ah ? See if yuh can get holt of her, Scotty."

The sheriff left Hashknife with Taylor, while he found Marion. The old man had little to say to Hashknife, and the conversation dragged heavily until the sheriff brought her in and introduced her to Hashknife.

" Did Tex offer to help us out ? " asked Taylor.

Marion nodded quickly.

" He did ; and I refused his offer. And he knows why I refused it, Dad."

" Gosh a'mighty—why ? "

" I can't tell you now."

" Uh-huh. Well, I jist wanted to know if he did. Mr. Hartley and his pardner offer to help yuh run the ranch at least until the round-up starts, and it shore looks generous—comin' from strangers."

" It certainly is generous ! " exclaimed Marion. " Dad, I think I can get Nanah to stay with me."

" That'll be fine. I'm much obliged to yuh,

Hartley, and I'll not be forgettin' this favour. We're shore up agin' a hard deal. How soon can yuh go out to the ranch ? "

" I broke a State record on saddlin' a bronc once," grinned Hashknife. " Our animals are in the livery stable, and I know Sleepy is plumb willin' to give up that bed at the hotel."

" Then we'll all ride out together," said Marion. " My horse is there too."

Hashknife found Sleepy at Moon's store and introduced him to Marion. Lee Barnhardt was there, and heard Hashknife explain to Sleepy that they were going to run the Double Bar 8. The lean-necked lawyer's brows elevated momentarily, and he wondered why Tex Alden hadn't handled that end of the deal.

Sleepy went with Marion to get the horses, while Hashknife secured paper and envelopes from Moon, and wrote a letter. Lee Barnhardt sat on a counter across the room, and wondered who this tall cowboy might be. Lee did not believe in philanthropy, and he wondered just why these two cowboys should offer to work the Double Bar 8 for nothing. He watched Hashknife, who hunched over the counter, taking much time over the composition of his letter.

Lee moved over to that counter and bought some tobacco he did not need. Hashknife sealed the letter and began directing the envelope. Lee walked slowly past him, getting a flash of the address on the letter, which was directed to Leesom & Brand, Attorneys at Law, Chicago.

If Lee Barnhardt expected to find any clue to Hashknife's identity, he could hardly find it in the address of a letter, but he smiled queerly as he walked to his office and sat down, twiddling his thumbs.

But it was not a pleasant smile, and his head sunk into his collar until the wattles of his wry-neck protruded. For about ten minutes he sat thus, totally absorbed in his own thoughts, which were finally broken by the entrance of Tex Alden, who had been depleting the stock of the Oasis saloon until he fairly reeked with alcoholic fumes.

" What do you know about them two fellers goin' out to the Taylor ranch ? " he demanded of Barnhardt.

" Eh ? " Lee looked up quickly. " Oh, yes. What about 'em ? "

" That's what I want to know."

" You're sore about something, ain't you, Tex ? "

" Yo're right, I am ! Who authorised them two punchers to run that place ? "

" Well, I didn't. It wasn't any of my business. Tex, you don't need to get drunk and come roaring into my office. I never sent them out there. It seems to me that Miss Taylor was perfectly willing to have them go out there. And they talked with old Apostle Paul. Don't hop me ; hop them."

" Hop —— ! " Tex leaned on the desk and glared at Barnhardt.

" Go to it, Tex. Hop anything you want to, but leave me out. Did you offer to run the ranch for her ? "

" I did ! "

Lee smiled at Tex's flushed face.

" What did she say ? "

" None of yore business ! "

" Mm-m-m-m ! Must have been a good reason."

" Who are these strange punchers ? "

Lee shook his head.

" How would I know ? They're going to run the Double Bar 8 for nothing. Rather charitable for a pair of strangers, don't you think, Tex ? "

" Too charitable."

" That's my opinion. But I don't know a thing against 'em."

" Know anythin' for 'em ? " bluntly.

" Not a thing, Tex. Marion is a mighty pretty girl, and——"

" Drop that ! " snapped Tex angrily. " Leave her out of it."

" Oh, all right. But she didn't talk as though she hated either of them. I heard her talking to them in Moon's store a while ago."

Tex's black eyes snapped angrily.

" I want to know a few things," he said evenly. " I'm no fool ! "

" Well, you'll not find out anything from me, because I don't know anything to tell you, Tex. I'm no judge of human nature, but I'd go easy with those two men. I don't think you can scare 'em. They've probably got a reason for running the Taylor ranch —for nothing."

" They can't scare me."

" They probably won't try," smiled Barnhardt.

" Anyway, they have no reason for trying to scare you. Tex, does their names mean anything to you ? "

" Their names ? Hartley and Stevens ? Not a thing."

" Ask Plenty Goode about it ? "

" What would he know about 'em, Lee ? "

" Do you remember one night out at the X Bar 6, just after Goode had hired out to you, and I was there ? We were talking about rustlers and horse-thieves, and Goode told us some of the things that happened in the Modoc country. He lived at Black Wells, I believe. Don't you remember the names now, Tex ? "

" Lee, I believe yo're right. What was it he called the tall one ? "

" Hashknife."

" That was it ! But are these the same men, Lee ? "

" I heard the tall one called by that name a while ago."

" Huh ! What do yuh reckon they're doin' over here ? "

Lee smiled crookedly.

" I dunno, Tex ; but it has probably got some-thing to do with the train robbery. And if I had held up that train, I'd sure hate to have these men on my trail. Ask Goode more about them, Tex."

Tex nodded slowly, thoughtfully. Suddenly he jerked ahead, his eyes boring into Barnhardt.

" Why should I worry about 'em ? They can't hang anythin' on to me ! "

" Oh, all right," sighed Lee. " I know I'd like to have that eight thousand dollars back from you. You better give it to me pretty quick, because I can't cover it up very long."

" Why can't yuh ? The round-up count can be long. You handle all the business for the X Bar 6, and you can add those cattle to your report. They don't know the sale was made."

" Compound a felony, eh ? Turn crook for you, Tex ? "

" Listen, Lee." Tex leaned across the desk and poked a finger at Lee's nose. " Yo're as crooked as a snake in a cactus patch. You'd double-cross yore best friend for a dollar. Don't swaller so hard ! I mean what I'm tellin' yuh. You told me about that Santa Rita pay-roll, because you wanted yore cut out of it, and yo're sore because yuh didn't get it.

" I haven't any eight thousand dollars. I ain't got no way to get eight thousand dollars. And what's more, I don't think I'd give it to yuh if I had it. Now, roll that up in some tar-paper and smoke it. Any old time you start playin' saint to my sins, yo're goin' to get in wrong. Now, think it over."

Tex surged away from the desk, and went out, scraping his spurs angrily, while Lee Barnhardt looked after him, gloomy-eyed, his lips compressed tightly. Finally he sighed and shook his head.

" Lee, your sins are finding you out," he said softly. " That poor fool is trying to bluff you—and he almost did."

CHAPTER X

HASHKNIFE AND SLEEPY, PHILANTHROPISTS

" THIS old place is sure pleasin' to the naked
eye," said Hashknife the following morning, while
Sleepy washed his face noisily at the old wash-
bench near the kitchen door. " I like this old patio,
Sleepy. Them walls were sure built to ward off
bullets."

" Yeah, and we're in a peaceable neighbour-
hood," grunted Sleepy, his eyes shut against the
sting of soap-suds, while he pawed awkwardly along
the wall, trying to locate the towel, which Hashknife
had deftly removed.

" Where's that towel ? " he roared. " Gimme
that, before I scalp yuh. Dang yuh, Hashknife,
you've got an idea of humour. Ow-w-w-w !
Please ! If I ever git m' eyes open ag'in, I'll scalp
yuh."

Sleepy danced violently, his dripping hands held
at right angles to his body.

" Whatsa idea of the ghost-dance ? " queried
Hashknife soberly. " The towel is there on the
wash-bench, where yuh left it."

This was palpably a falsehood, but Sleepy pawed
his way to the bench, found the towel, and wiped
his burning eyes.

" You hadn't ought to use laundry soap in yore eyes," said Hashknife reprovingly. "Whatcha cryin' about ? "

" You stole that towel ! Yeah, yuh did ! Oh, well ! " Sleepy shrugged his shoulders. " A feller that ain't got no more sense than to throw in with a danged——"

" Halt ! " snorted Hashknife. " Say it, and I'll wash out yore mouth, Sleepy."

" Oh, yuh will ! " Sleepy glared at Hashknife, who was in line with the kitchen door, where Marion stood, laughing.

" Ex-cuse me, Miss Taylor," said Sleepy. " If you'd lived with Hashknife—uh—I mean, if you——" Sleepy floundered and wiped his eyes.

" You'll excuse him, Miss Taylor," said Hashknife seriously. " He ain't very bright. Every once in a while he gets a dirty look in his eyes, and has to wash 'em out, yuh see. As a friend he's all right, but when yuh want mental companionship, I'd as soon have that burro yuh call Apollo."

Marion laughed, and invited them in to breakfast. She introduced them to Nanah, a portly Indian woman, whom Sleepy dubbed " Carrie Nation," because she held a hatchet in her left hand, while she shook hands with the other.

" She's related to Peeler," explained Marion.

" Relate by marriage," said Nanah solemnly, as if to amend Marion's statement.

" Nephew ? " asked Hashknife, helping himself to a stack of hot-cakes.

" Son," said Nanah seriously.

" Relate by marriage ! " exploded Sleepy.

Nanah did not smile. She spilled more batter on the griddle, examining the pitcher closely, as she glanced at Hashknife's plate, possibly fearing she had underestimated their hot-cake ability, and said :—

" Somebody say Peeler rob train. —— lie ! Too lazy."

" And that's the most perfect alibi I ever heard," laughed Hashknife. " Nanah, I'll bet any jury in Blue Wells would turn him loose on that kind of evidence."

" What do you think of the case ? " asked Marion.

Hashknife shook his head.

" I dunno, Miss Taylor. It kinda looks to me as though the sheriff had kinda gone off half-cocked. That old judge ought to be restin' in a cemetery. I dunno how any community could stand for an old mummy like him. He ain't human. There ain't nothin' against 'em, except that darned dog, and the fact they were not home that night."

" But they surely couldn't convict on that evidence."

" Mm-m-m-m-m ! " Hashknife masticated thoughtfully. " I dunno. I've seen queer things happen. I 'member a case where one man was suin' another for stealin' his wife, and the cow-jury brought in a verdict of manslaughter against the prosecutin' attorney."

" A-a-a-aw, don't lie like that ! " protested Sleepy. " You never seen nothin' of the kind."

" Well, I've seen things just about as bad. I don't trust humanity—not cow-jury humanity. If I was goin' to win that case, I'd do it out of court, Miss Taylor."

" But how could that be done ? " asked Marion eagerly.

" Find the men that done the job."

" An easy thing to think about," observed Sleepy, leaning back to let Nanah slide a pile of hot cakes on his plate.

" But the sheriff won't do anything now," said Marion. " He feels that he has done his duty."

" Prob'ly a good thing he won't," grinned Hashknife. " Any man that wears a moustache like Olson does, couldn't find his own socks inside his boots. That man has all gone to hair."

" Samson wore long hair," reminded Sleepy. " He was strong."

" Strong—yea-a-ah ! But did he have any brains ? He didn't. If he had any brains he wouldn't have let that woman monkey around him with a pair of shears. Just to prove that he was thick—he slept through the hair-cuttin'. Can yuh imagine that ? "

" I think Wade, the railroad detective, was more responsible for the arrests than Olson was," said Marion.

" I've seen him," nodded Hashknife. " He's one of them kinda jiggers that don't care whether he gets the guilty man or not, just so he gets somebody. That feller used to be a policeman in Los Angeles. They take the uniform off a policeman— and he's a detective.

" Do yuh know that the idea of numberin' houses in a city was started by a police department ? It was. Their officers was always gettin' into the wrong houses ; so they numbered 'em. Nanah, you make gosh-awful good hot cakes. Yuh do so. You Navajo ? "

Nanah nodded quickly.

" Do you speak Navajo ? " asked Marion.

Hashknife shook his head.

" Nope. Speak a little Nez Perce, Flathead, Sioux, English, and Profane. Yuh have a wear a rag around yore head to learn Navajo."

" And pack a snake around in yore teeth," added Sleepy.

Marion laughed at the expression of Nanah's face.

" I not bite snake," declared the squaw seriously.

" That's right," said Hashknife. " Doncha do it, Nanah."

They shoved back from the table and rolled cigarettes, while Nanah and Marion cleared away the dishes.

" If you were going to try and find the men who held up that train—where would you look ? " asked Marion.

Hashknife smiled over his cigarette.

" That's hard to say. I'd have to do a little addition, subtraction, and division. Didja ever get far enough in school to work on problems where they let X equal the missin' numbers ? "

Marion smiled.

" Yes, I have, Mr. Hartley."

" Well, then, don't call me mister. My name's Hashknife. Now that yuh know me well enough to call me Hashknife, I'd say that I'd let about four X's equal the missin' bandits, and work out the problem from there. We've got the dog Workin' backwards from a dog, yuh ought to get quite a lot.

" In the beginnin', I'd like to ask yuh what yuh know about a feller who is workin' for the AK outfit who is named Jimmy Legg."

" James Eaton Legg," said Marion solemnly. " He said it sounded like a cannibal. I don't know a thing about him, except that he came to Blue Wells the night of the robbery. Johnny Grant took a liking to him, and took him out to the AK, where he's been falling off horses ever since. He says he's going to learn to be a cowboy, if he lives long enough—and that's all I know about him."

" Not much," mused Hashknife. " Nice boy ? "

" Certainly he's nice," said Marion, without hesitation.

" I s'pose so," smiled Hashknife. " Bein' as yo're the boss of this outfit, suppose yuh tell us what yuh want done to-day."

" I don't know," she confessed. " Suppose you spend the day in getting used to the place."

" All right. Mebbe we'll corral a few horses and look 'em over. If we handle the round-up for the Double Bar 8, we're goin' to need a remuda."

" Sure. Suppose you ride back to Blue Wells some time to-day and bring back the three that are in the livery stable. We forgot them."

" That's right. How about the chuck-wagon ? "

" Oh, I forgot about that. We have always used the X Bar 6 outfit wagons. Tex Alden has always insisted that our outfit was too small to run their own chuck-wagon. But this year——"

Marion's pause was significant. Hashknife realised that everything was not right between the Taylor family and Alden.

" He didn't invite yuh to share his chuck, eh ? "

Marion shook her head slowly.

" I guess we'll get along all right."

" Y'betcha," warmly. " We'll kinda look things over, Miss Taylor."

" And now that we're well enough acquainted for you to call me Marion——"

" Oh, all right," laughed Hashknife.

He joined Sleepy in the patio, and they inspected the stables and corrals, with Apollo following them like a dog, trying to nip the brims of their hats.

It was possibly half an hour later that Lee Barnhardt rode in at the ranch, and the Blue Wells attorney was a sight for sore eyes. His mount was a sway-backed sorrel, with a long neck and a whispy tail. Barnhardt did not wear chaps, and the action of the horse had wrinkled his trousers, until the bottoms were up to his knees, showing an expanse of skinny leg and a pair of mismated socks. On his head he wore a sombrero, which was too small for him, and a flannel shirt, so large around the neck that one could easily catch a glimpse of his collar-bone.

He nodded pleasantly to Hashknife and Sleepy,

and dismounted, allowing his trousers to resume a normal attitude toward his legs.

" I just rode out to see how things were going," he explained. " I spoke to Mr. Taylor about it."

" Well, yuh don't need to apologise," grinned Hashknife. " Of course yuh got here pretty early in the mornin' to find anythin' goin' on. That's quite a bronc you've got."

" Yes ; he's all right. Not much for looks, but reliable. Is Miss Taylor at home ? "

" I think you'll find her in the house."

" Thank you."

Barnhardt dusted off his clothes with a flap of his hands, and headed toward the house, while Hashknife and Sleepy grinned at each other.

" That," said Hashknife seriously, " is the attorney."

" I'm disappointed," said Sleepy seriously.

" Yuh don't need to be, Sleepy. Hallo ! Here comes the next chapter."

Jimmy Legg had arrived at the Double Bar 8 with his head swathed in bandages, his sombrero cocked at an angle. He slid out of his saddle, hitched up his belt, and gazed soberly at the two cowboys.

" Hallo," he said.

" How's the head ? " asked Hashknife.

" Gee, it sure was sore this morning. I didn't sleep much last night. I guess I was scared." Jimmy grinned widely. " Got to thinking how close I came to getting me a harp. Honest, it was an awful dream. You see, I'm not musical at all."

The two cowboys grinned with Jimmy. He looked at the lawyer's horse quizzically.

"Who rides that thing?" he asked.

"An attorney from Blue Wells," said Hashknife.

"Oh, Lee Barnhardt? Well," Jimmy hitched up his belt, "it looks like him. They've both got the same shape neck."

"Yuh hadn't ought to make fun of a horse," said Sleepy.

"No, I suppose not. Really, I shouldn't make fun of anybody. I ought to put in most of my time being thankful I'm alive. I am, too. I've got to go and have the doctor dress my head, but I thought I'd stop and see Miss Taylor. She's going to need some help around here, and I thought I'd offer my services. The AK really don't need me."

"What can you do?" asked Hashknife.

Jimmy shuffled his feet.

"Well," he said slowly, "I really don't know. Unless, of course, she has some horses that need to have some one fall off them. Johnny Grant says I'm the best he has ever seen. He says if you're a champion rider there's always a dispute over it. But if you're a champion faller-off, you've got a cinch title."

The two cowboys laughed at Jimmy, or rather, with him.

"Can yuh handle a rope?" asked Hashknife.

"Not on a horse. There's too many things to remember. I always fall off, trying to keep from tripping my own horse. On the ground, I'm pretty good. Eskimo says I can heat a branding-iron

handle hotter than anybody he ever seen. And
that about lets me out, I guess."

" Well, yo're honest about it, anyway," laughed
Sleepy. " If yuh live long enough, you'll prob'ly
be a top-hand about the time they stop raisin'
cattle and start on sugar-beets."

" I'd have an even chance with the rest of the
cowboys at raising sugar-beets, I suppose."

" You sure are an optimist, pardner," laughed
Hashknife. " I hope Miss Taylor can use yuh.
We need an optimist around us."

" Fine," grinned Jimmy. " And I'd learn just
as much about being a cowboy."

" And maybe live longer," said Sleepy. " Things
that might make others shoot—make us laugh.
You better tie up yore bronc."

Jimmy tied his horse to a ring in the patio wall,
and they went inside the patio, where they found
Marion and Barnhardt. She shook hands with
Jimmy, who protested that he was better than he
ever was. Barnhardt looked him over coldly, but
no one bothered to introduce them.

" I'm looking for a job," laughed Jimmy. " I
told Mr. Bonnette that I was going to offer my
services to you, and he said it would be all right
with him. He was very nice about it."

" He knows the salary," said Hashknife. " We
split it three ways."

" Well, that's mighty nice of you, Jimmy," said
Marion.

" Don't mention it, Marion."

Barnhardt cleared his throat raspingly. He

wanted to voice an objection, but had none. Hash-knife's eyes were smiling, but his mouth was serious, as he watched the lawyer's face.

"I think we are being well taken care of, Mr. Barnhardt," said Marion, her eyes dancing.

"Oh, hu—er—yes, indeed." Barnhardt mopped his face with a silk handkerchief. "Very, very well, Miss Taylor. I—I guess I will be going along."

"Come again," said Hashknife cordially.

Barnhardt flashed a glance at him, as he held out his hand to Marion.

They walked to the patio gate and watched Barn-hardt ride away, sitting stiffly in his saddle, his horse trotting, every jerk of which drew Barnhardt's trousers up nearer his knees, and caused his ill-fitting sombrero to shift from side to side.

"Looks like the joker in a deck of playin'-cards," observed Sleepy.

"He means well, I think," said Marion, as they turned back.

"Means well to Lee Barnhardt," smiled Hash-knife.

"I don't like him," said Jimmy. "Oh, it isn't because of anything he has ever done to me," he hastened to say. "But it is just something about him that—well, I don't like him."

"Shall we show our new member to the bunk-house?" asked Hashknife. "I like him a lot better since I've heard he don't like lawyers."

"Oh, my remark does not cover the entire pro-fession," said Jimmy quickly.

Marion laughed and went into the house, while

Hashknife and Sleepy introduced Jimmy to the bunk-house. They sat down and rolled cigarettes. Jimmy was not very adept, but he managed to make his own smoke.

" You know Miss Taylor pretty well, don'tcha ? " asked Hashknife.

Jimmy coloured quickly.

" Well, not awful well."

" Well enough to call her Marion."

" She asked me to call her that. But that's all right, isn't it ? "

" It's all right with me. But it got under the hide of that lawyer."

" It's none of his business."

" No-o-o, I suppose not, Jimmy. Have you any idea who shot yuh ? "

Jimmy started to speak, changed his mind, and shook his head.

" I heard," said Hashknife slowly, " that two prominent young men in this community had declared their intentions of marryin' this young lady."

" Oh, I know that," said Jimmy quickly. " Tex Alden and Chet Le Moyne. But that doesn't make any difference to me."

" I see," Hashknife grinned widely. " You'll make it a three-cornered affair, eh ? "

" Not at all. You see, I—I hardly know the lady. She was nice to me, and I appreciate it. But I never said I wanted to marry her."

" You've met Chet Le Moyne ? "

" Yes, I've met him. We were introduced at the Oasis saloon."

" Where did you meet Tex Alden ? "

" I never was introduced to him, but I—I talked to him here."

" Yeah ? And he told yuh to keep away, didn't he ? "

Jimmy looked at Hashknife in amazement.

" Why, how did you know that ? "

" I didn't," smiled Hashknife. " I knew you'd correct me if I was wrong."

Jimmy rubbed his nose and grinned foolishly.

" That's one way of finding out, I suppose. Yes, he did tell me to keep away from here."

" And that night you got shot."

" Gee ! Do you think he shot me ? "

Hashknife smiled softly over the manufacture of another cigarette, but did not answer.

" What do you think I ought to do ? " queried Jimmy.

" Just forget it," replied Hashknife. " You don't know anything about it, Jimmy."

" I know, but——" Jimmy hesitated awkwardly. " But he—whoever fired that shot—wanted to kill me, didn't they ? Don't you suppose they'll try again ? "

" Undoubtedly."

" Gee, that puts me in a fine position ! "

" Yea-a-ah, it does. You ought to grab a train and high-tail it out of this country."

Jimmy thought it over seriously, the smoke from his cigarette drifting up into his eyes.

" No," he said finally, " I won't go. I've never injured any one, and I'm not going to run away."

"And take chances on bein' killed ? "

Jimmy nodded.

" Yes ; it's all right. I might be lucky."

Hashknife held out his hand to Jimmy, as he said:—

" Young man, you belong. I wouldn't blame yuh if yuh ran away. We're just a pair of ordinary human beings, but we're backin' yore play."

" Gee, that's nice of you ! I'm not much good —not alone. I didn't come here with the idea of becoming a gunman, but I wish somebody would show me something about a revolver. It tries to jump out of my hand every time I shoot it, and I can't hit a five-gallon can at ten feet. Really, a fellow should know something about a gun—if somebody is trying to kill him."

" It might come in handy," smiled Hashknife. " Neither of us are good shots, but we can show you how to point a gun."

" Fine ! And to draw one real fast, like Johnny Grant can ? "

" I've never seen Johnny Grant draw a gun. I've found that it isn't all in the speed. Too much speed wastes the first shot. Never reach for a gun unless you mean to use it, and when you do reach, draw and shoot deliberately. Split-second gunmen don't hit anythin'. And another thing, Jimmy—don't shoot unless yo're in the right. Bein' right to start with will win nine times out of ten. You know it and the other man knows it."

" I think I know what you mean, Mr. Hartley."

" I'm glad yuh do—and my name's Hashknife— to them that belong."

Jimmy grinned widely. It was the first time that any one had even intimated that he might " belong," and his heart filled with gratitude toward this tall, serious-faced cowboy, who had admitted him to the brotherhood of cowpunchers.

" But you'll never make a cowpuncher out of yourself by gettin' pitched off every bronc yuh see," declared Sleepy. " Bein' a cow-hand don't necessarily mean that yuh can ride anythin' that wears hair. Nobody's goin' to blame yuh, if yuh don't ride bad ones. That's only a small part of the business—the fool part, Jimmy."

" I suppose you're right," admitted Jimmy. " I wasn't born to ride buckers. I was just wondering how you two men happened to be cowboys."

" Circumstance, I reckon," said Hashknife. " I was born on the Milk River, in Montana. My dad was a preacher, Jimmy. Not the kind of a preacher you've known. He wore overalls and boots, and when he wasn't ridin' from place to place, packin' his gospel, he was workin' at somethin' else to make a livin' for the family, because preachin' didn't pay dividends.

" There was six of us kids, and I was the oldest; which meant that I was shiftin' for myself when I was twelve. I naturally didn't get over-educated. But I competed against men, and they taught me things. There wasn't anythin' to do in that country, except punchin' cows; so I naturally learned the business.

" In fact, I was about eighteen years old before I knew there was anythin' else in the world. Then

I started driftin', learnin', and fightin' my way
I got whipped a lot of times, but I learned a lot
of things ; some of it from books, but a lot more
from humanity. It's been a hard school, Jimmy—
and it still is ; a school where yuh never graduate."

" I never thought of the world in that way,
Hashknife."

" That's the way she is," declared Sleepy. " I
got off in about the same way Hashknife did.
My folks wanted to honour Idaho ; so they moved
over near Pocatello before I was born. I went to
school, when they could find a man who was brave
enough to teach the risin' sons—which wasn't no
ways regular. The last teacher we had was a horse-
thief, and he almost got me mixed up with him in
a deal.

" I jist kinda growed up, got some wild-eyed
ideas, and follered a bunch of geese South. I had
a lot of corners on me, and inside of three years
I had 'em all knocked off. In three years more I
had hollers where there used to be bumps. About
that time I decided that there was a lot of other
folks in the world ; so I sawed off my horns and
held my elbows close to my sides, when I went
through a crowd. I eventually drifted to the
Hashknife outfit, where I finds my pardner. I
dunno just how or why he picked up with me,
but we've been together ever since."

" I felt sorry for yuh," said Hashknife solemnly.

" Yeah, and I've felt sorry for myself ever since."

From out in the patio came the raucous bray of
Apollo, as if he had joined the laugh. The three

men sauntered out into the patio, where Apollo was nosing around in a water-bucket. He looked them over suspiciously and angled crab-wise toward Sleepy, who was wise in the ways of a burro.

" Git away from me, yuh relic ! " snorted Sleepy, slapping at the burro with his hat. Marion came from the house, laughing at Sleepy's antics, and they grouped together at the well.

" Apollo is a family heirloom," laughed Marion. " No man knows his age. The Indians say he was here when they came, and he has never grown old, except in appearance."

Marion put one arm over the burro's neck and rubbed his nose with her hand.

" He loves me," she said.

" And I heard a man say once that a burro didn't have any sense," smiled Hashknife.

Marion coloured slightly.

" They're the wisest of animals," declared Sleepy.

Came the sharp thud of a blow, as if something had struck the burro with a heavy impact, and the ancient animal dropped as if its legs had been suddenly yanked from under its body. In fact, its fall was so sudden that Marion jerked forward, lost her balance, and fell sprawling across its neck.

And as she fell, from somewhere back in the hills came the report of a rifle shot. It was so sudden, so unexpected, that no one moved for a moment. Then Hashknife flung himself forward, grasped Marion in his arms, and ran back to the shelter of the bunk-house, with Sleepy and Jimmy following.

They stopped against the bunk-house door, staring at each other. Marion was dazed but unhurt.

" What was it ? " she asked.

" Yo're not hurt ? " asked Hashknife anxiously.

" I'm not hurt. I—I just fell down. But what——"

" Good gosh, that sure was a close one ! " exclaimed Sleepy. " Some dirty coyote——"

" Shot at me," finished Jimmy nervously. "That bullet went past my ear—I felt it."

" But—but——" faltered Marion.

" Stay where yuh are," cautioned Hashknife.

He ran into the bunk-house, and came out in a minute, stuffing cartridges into the loading-gate of one of the ranch rifles.

" Oh, be careful about showing yourself," cautioned Marion.

" Thanks," grinned Hashknife.

He moved along the patio wall, slipped out through the gate, while Sleepy took a rifle from the bunk-house, swearing disgustedly over the fact that Hashknife had taken all the cartridges.

" It came from the hill back of us," said Marion. " Poor old Apollo ! "

" Yea, he's a goner," said Sleepy softly. " Well, that's about all yuh ever could do to make him die. If old age was ever goin' to kill him, he'd 'a' died forty years ago."

There were tears in Marion's eyes as she looked at the sprawling figure of the ancient burro. Worse than useless, he had always been a part of the Double Bar 8. It was the razing of a landmark.

Suddenly the ancient one shuddered, lifted its misshapen head and goggled foolishly. Then it got slowly to unsteady legs, staggered a few feet, thrust out its head, opened a cavernous mouth, which showed a few crooked teeth, and brayed defiance to all rifle-shooting bushwhackers.

" My —— ! " snorted Sleepy. " A rifle can't even kill it ! "

Marion was laughing and crying alternately, and Sleepy grasped her by the arm to prevent her from going out to the burro.

" It just creased him," explained Sleepy. " See where that blood streak runs down his neck ? That bullet went through his neck just over the vertebræ, knocked him plumb out for a while, but he's as good as ever now."

Apollo looked reproachfully at Sleepy, stretched his neck tentatively, and moved over to the shade of the wall, evidently none the worse for his experience.

When Hashknife left the patio gate he hugged the wall, circling to the rear of the bunk-house, from where he ran to the stable. He decided that the shot had been fired from a point on the hill, near the upper end of a small cañon. It was about the only spot on that side where a man could get elevation enough to enable him to see the centre of the patio.

There was plenty of brush on the slope behind the stable ; brush tall enough to conceal him from any one on the slope ; so Hashknife did not hesitate to head directly for the spot he had in mind. There was no more shooting, but Hashknife could

not be sure that the bushwhacker had not seen
him start from the patio ; so when he was half-
way up to the break of the cañon, he went carefully.
taking advantage of the heaviest cover in sight.

Hashknife realised his own danger. It was
almost impossible for him to move without making
a noise in the dry brush. And he did not know
what moment a bullet might search him out.
Working to the right, he came to the cañon-rim,
where he sprawled under a bush, listening closely.

Near him a flock of quail scurried about in the
brush, their peculiar call, ventriloquistic, " Sit
right there ! " echoing back from the cañon-walls.
One of them passed within inches of the rifle muzzle,
a nervously jerking handful of blue and bronze,
evidently puzzled at this sprawled figure of a human,
which did not move.

The quail were working up the slope. Peering
beneath the brush, Hashknife could see the little
blue fellows running from cover to cover, while
their calling became more faint. Hashknife slid
farther out on the rim, and was about to get to his
feet, when he saw the flock of quail whir up from
the brush, and come hurtling down the cañon,
swinging in below him, scattering badly, and
beginning their warning cries again.

Something or somebody had disturbed them.
Then he heard the sound of something coming
down through the brush toward him. He got to
his haunches, swinging his rifle into position as a
horse and rider broke through the brush, almost
against him.

The black horse snorted wildly, as Hashknife arose, covering the rider with the rifle. The man jerked back and his hands went above his head, while the horse surged back. The rider was of medium height, slightly gray, his bronzed face heavily lined, one cheek bulged with a chew of tobacco. He quieted the horse, spat explosively and shut one eye as he looked down at Hashknife.

" Well ? " he said, rather defiantly.

" Not so well," said Hashknife coldly.

He circled the horse, but there was no rifle in sight.

" What's the idea ? " queried the man.

"" That's what I want to know. Who are you, pardner ? "

" M' name's Goode. G-o-o-d-e. Called 'Plenty.'"

" Yeah ? Good rifle shot ? "

" Fair."

" Uh-huh," Hashknife considered Mr. Goode. He was not a soft-looking person.

" Of course, it's none of my business, but I'm just curious to know who, or which one of us, you tried to kill a while ago, Mr. Goode ? "

" Me ? " Goode spat thoughtfully. " That's a queer question, my friend with the cocked Winchester. 'S far as I remember, I ain't tried to kill anybody for a long time."

" No-o-o-o ? " drawled Hashknife. " I hate to call a man a liar."

" Prob'ly," dryly. " I hate to be called one, when I've got my hands in the air."

" Sure. Yuh might care to tell me how yuh happen to be right here about this time."

" Cinch. I'm from the X Bar 6 outfit. Me and Ed Gast was back toward Yaller Horn mesa to-day, and when we're on our way back I decides to ride down to the Double Bar 8. Ed went on to Blue Wells ; so I cuts a straight line for here. Satisfied ? "

" But not contented," said Hashknife. " Just why didja want to come to the Double Bar 8 ? You know well the three men from that ranch are in jail at Blue Wells."

" Oh, I knowed that all right. But I wanted to get a look at the two men who are runnin' the place."

" Get a look at 'em, eh ? "

Goode grinned widely, showing his tobacco-stained teeth.

" I reckon yo're one of em, stranger. Yuh see, I lived at Black Wells when you and yore pardner cleaned up the Modoc trouble, and I heard a lot about yuh. I've always wanted to thank yore pardner for killin' Jud Mahley. It saved me a ca'tridge."

Hashknife studied the face of the ex-Black Wells cowboy, but the man seemed sincere.

" I want to believe yuh, Goode. But a while ago somebody fired a rifle up here, and the bullet almost killed a woman in the Double Bar 8 patio."

Goode's eyes narrowed.

" And yuh thought I done it, Hartley ? "

" I found yuh here."

" Yeah, that's true. I heard the shot. It wasn't long ago. But a shot don't mean anythin'. I scared up a flock of quail back there on the hill, and I jist wondered if somebody hadn't been out tryin' to get a meal of 'em."

Hashknife lowered his gun and let down the hammer.

" I'm takin' you at yore word, Goode," he said. " There's got to be a reason for that shot—and I don't reckon you've got one."

" Well, I sure ain't, Hartley. Any old time I go bushwhackin', it won't be you, nor any of yore friends."

" Well, that's sure thoughtful of yuh. Do yuh know Miss Taylor ? "

" Know who she is. Tex Alden intended to send me and one of the other boys down here to run this ranch, but when you boys took it, I reckon he changed his mind."

" It didn't make him mad, did it, Goode ? "

Goode looked curiously at Hashknife, his lips pursed thoughtfully.

" Well, it hadn't ought to," he said slowly.

Hashknife nodded. He liked Goode for that remark.

" We might as well go down to the ranch-house," suggested Hashknife. " I reckon the shootin' is all over."

" I hope t' gosh it is, Hartley. That's nasty business."

They went to the ranch-house, where Hashknife introduced Goode to Sleepy and Jimmy. Marion had gone into the house, but came out a few minutes later and was introduced. Hashknife explained how he had met Goode.

It was possibly a half an hour later that Goode rode away. His explanation of how he happened to be there on the hill so soon after the shooting did not satisfy Sleepy.

"That jigger's eyes are hard," declared Sleepy. "Jist like moss-agate. And he's from Black Wells, Hashknife."

"I *sabe* that," smiled Hashknife. "But I don't think he did fire that shot. He don't look like a hired killer, and it's a cinch he ain't got no personal reason for killin' any of us."

"Ain't he?" Sleepy smiled wisely. "Just suppose Mr. Goode is one of that gang of train robbers? He knows what we done in the Modoc country. Figure it out for yourself."

Hashknife nodded seriously.

"Yeah, that might be true. Mebbe he thinks we're here to work on that case. I hate to get fooled on humanity, Sleepy. That feller may be awful slick. He's either innocent, or smooth as satin, because he sure had an alibi on the end of his tongue."

"But he didn't have any rifle," said Jimmy.

"A rifle is easy to hide," said Sleepy, shaking his head. "Nossir, I'd look out for Mr. Goode."

"But that shot was fired at me." Jimmy was not to be denied of his thrill. "It went right past my ear."

"And why would Goode shoot at Jimmy?" questioned Marion.

Hashknife laughed, and picked some of the burrs off his knees.

" We've got to get an answer-book, folks. I'm
glad that the heirloom was only creased. But from
now on we've got to be mighty careful. Unless I'm
mistaken, that shot was only a beginnin'."

" Do you think you ought to stay here ? " asked
Marion nervously. " I mean, to take a chance
on your lives, just to help me out ? "

Hashknife looked at Jimmy, who dug his heel
savagely in the hard ground, appearing ill at ease.
Finally he looked up, noticing that both Hashknife
and Sleepy were waiting for him to answer Marion's
question.

" Well," he said, " as far as I'm concerned, I'll
stay."

" Three times—and out," said Hashknife softly.
" They've tried twice, Jimmy."

" I know," seriously. " But," he grinned and
peeled some sunburn off his nose, " I'm beginnin'
to think that you never will die until your time
comes."

" And that thought will sure help yuh win a
lot of fights where the odds are all against yuh,
Jimmy," said Hashknife.

" Are you a fatalist ? " asked Marion.

" Well," grinned Hashknife, " if I wasn't, I'd
'a' been scared to death years ago."

" I would like to hear about that Modoc affair,"
said Jimmy.

Hashknife shook his head quickly.

" No, Jimmy. It wasn't anything. Goode kinda
got things twisted. I hope Carrie Nation gets some
food on the table pretty soon."

It was like Hashknife to refuse to tell of things they had done. After he and Sleepy Stevens had joined forces and left the Hashknife outfit, fate seemed to throw them into troubled waters. Hashknife was either blessed or cursed with an analytical mind. A range mystery was food and drink to him. Sleepy's mind ran in normal channels, but he loved to roam, and his love of adventure, fearlessness in the face of danger, made him a valuable ally to Hashknife.

So for a number of years their trail had led them where the cattle roamed, working on mysteries ; more often than not, working for the sheer love of the thing, rather than for pay. At times they had stepped out of a pall of powder smoke, mounted their horses, and rode away ahead of the thanks of those whose future had been made more bright by their coming.

" Soldiers of fortune," a man had called them.

" Cowpunchers of disaster," corrected Hashknife.

And in all their wanderings, the thing uppermost in their minds was to find the spot where they might be satisfied to settle down and live a peaceful life ; both of them realising all the while that they would never be satisfied with peace. Always, the other side of the hill called to them— the irresistible call of the open, of the strange places, which is always answered by men who can't sit still.

CHAPTER XI

AFTER Goode rode back to Blue Wells he met Leo Barnhardt, who was taking a drink at the Oasis, and Goode, who was also drinking, told him of his visit to the Double Bar 8, and of the mysterious shot. The lawyer was naturally interested, and questioned Goode closely, but Goode knew nothing of who had fired the shot.

"I met Hartley and Stevens," offered Goode. "They're the same two jiggers that cleaned up that Modoc job."

"Detectives?" asked Barnhardt.

"Oh, I dunno about that part of it. But that ain't the only job they ever cleaned up. There's a lot more behind that one, and I'll betcha they've not been idle since then. I'm wonderin' what they're doin' here."

"Perhaps they're working on that train robbery."

"Pshaw, that might be it. I'll buy a drink, Barnhardt."

On his way back to the office Barnhardt met Le Moyne.

"Whatever happened to that detective the Santa Rita was going to put on that robbery?" asked Barnhardt.

Le Moyne smiled.

" Why, I guess the company didn't think it was worth while, as long as you folks had jailed some one for doing the job."

Barnhardt laughed softly, knowingly.

" That's all right, Chet. But when you hire detectives, why don't you get men whose reputations are not so well known ? "

Le Moyne looked him over coldly.

" What do you mean, Lee ? "

" Oh, I respect your secrecy. But really, Hartley and Stevens are too well known to do much good."

" Eh ? " Le Moyne frowned heavily. " Those two men at the Taylor ranch ? "

" Sure. The two best man hunters you could have hired. But it's a case of them being too well known."

" Yeah ? " Le Moyne smiled thinly. " Too well known, eh ? But don't blame me—I'm not the Santa Rita company."

" That's true."

" Personally, I know nothing about their reputation, Lee."

" You don't ? Well, I don't know very much, but I do know that they've never lost a case. I'd hate to have them on my trail."

" Well," Le Moyne shrugged his shapely shoulders, " it seems as though we had hired two very good men, Lee."

" You have." Barnhardt laughed and grew confidential. " Tex Alden is as sore as a boil. He didn't want them two men to stay at the ranch. He intended to run the ranch himself."

"He did, eh?" Le Moyne scowled. "Yeah, I suppose he would. I'm glad he missed out on that. And I'm glad the sheriff and the railroad detective had to make that arrest. It rather lets me out of any blame in the matter, you see."

"Certainly."

"They've got plenty of help at the Double Bar 8," said Barnhardt, after a pause. "That tenderfoot, Jimmy Legg, who was at the AK ranch, has volunteered his services. Tex sure is sore at him."

"Sore at Legg? What for?"

"Well, Tex thinks Marion pays too much attention to Legg."

"Well, does she?"

"I don't know, Chet. She calls him Jimmy, and he calls her Marion."

"Does, eh? Say, Lee, where did that fellow come from?"

"Nobody seems to know. He tramped in here the night of the hold-up. He said the train passed him. I can't quite figure him out. I've talked with Scotty Olson and Al Porter about him, and they're not quite sure what he is. He's not a bad looking fellow, and I think he has a way with women."

"What do you mean by that?"

"Well, you know, Chet; sort of a way of talking."

"Yea-a-ah, I guess I know what you mean," sighed Le Moyne. "I'll see you later, Lee."

Barnhardt went back to his office, glowing with the self-satisfaction that comes to men who love to gossip. Le Moyne met Goode at the Oasis, and Goode was carrying just a little too much liquor. Goode happened to be extolling Hashknife and Sleepy to the bartender, who evidently didn't care a bit about it.

" I tell yuh, they're invin-shi-ble," he declared. " Bes' pair of two-handed fighters on earth. Betcha odds, tha's what'll do."

" Hallo, Plenty," said Le Moyne.

Goode goggled at Le Moyne.

" Howza paymashter ? Whatcha usin' f'r money these days, Chet ? "

" Good yellow gold, Plenty. What do you want to bet on ? "

" Don't get him started," advised the bartender. " He's drunk. Wants to bet odds that Hartley and Stevens will find the men who robbed your pay-roll."

Le Moyne laughed and bought a drink.for every one at the bar.

" I'm tellin' yuh," declared Goode. " 'F they was after me, I'd run like ——, and pray every jump."

" Bad men, eh ? " asked Le Moyne, laughing.

" Wors' you ever sheen ! Gun-shootin' mind-readers. Yesshir. Oh, you'll shee."

He pointed a wavering finger in the direction of the bartender.

" Betcha oddsh. Betcha anythin'——"

Goode waved his arm, as if to encompass every-thing, and sat down on the bar-rail, where he began snoring.

" Can't stand much," said the bartender. " Give him ten drinks of hooch, and he's plumb gone. Know anythin' about Hartley and Stevens ? "

Le Moyne smiled and his brows lifted slightly.

" You knew the Santa Rita had detectives on the case, didn't you ? "

" Oh, I did hear they was goin' to. What'll yuh drink, Chet ? "

" Same thing. I wonder where Goode found out so much about those two men ? "

" I don't know. He's been out to the Double Bar 8 to see 'em, and when he came back he met Al Porter here. They had a few shots of hooch, and Goode told Al all about 'em. The more drinks he took, the more he told. After Al went away, Barnhardt came in, and Goode told it all over again. When Barnhardt went out, I was the victim. You're lucky he went to sleep."

" I suppose I am," laughed Le Moyne. " It appears that the Double Bar 8 is well taken care of right now. Did any one find out who shot that tenderfoot kid the other night ? "

" Never tried to, I reckon. The kid went back to the AK."

" He's over at the Taylor place now."

" Is that so ? "

" That's what I heard."

" Oh, sure ; I heard that too. You heard about somebody takin' a shot at the gang at the Double Bar 8, didn't yuh ? "

Le Moyne hadn't ; so the bartender told him what he had heard Goode tell Barnhardt. It was interesting to Le Moyne, inasmuch as the bullet nearly struck Marion.

"That sure beats everything!" snorted Le Moyne. "What kind of a country is this getting to be? I wonder," he squinted thoughtfully, "if that shot was fired at Legg, the tenderfoot?"

"Might have been. What'll yuh have, Chet?"

"Nothing; I've had enough."

Le Moyne turned his back to the bar, while he rolled and lighted a cigarette, his eyes thoughtful. Scotty Olson came in and spoke to Le Moyne as he walked past, but the handsome paymaster of the Santa Rita did not reply. Finally he walked out, mounted his horse, and rode away.

The sheriff came back to the bar.

"What's the matter with Le Moyne?" he asked of the bartender.

"I dunno." The bartender rested his elbows on the bar, chewing on his cigar. "I told him about the bushwhacker out at the Double Bar 8 almost killin' Marion Taylor, and I suppose Le Moyne is sore about it."

"Al Porter was tellin' me about it," nodded the sheriff. "I don't *sabe* it."

"You'd be a wonder if yuh did, Scotty. This country is getting pretty salty, don'tcha know it? First a train robbery, then an attempted murder on the main street, and now they're shootin' from the hills."

"And what for?" wailed the sheriff. "I do hate a mystery!"

"Sure yuh do, Scotty. What'll yuh drink?

See-gar ? Sure. These ought to be good. Paid five dollars for that box of 'em three years ago. Pretty dry ? Well, you'd be dry too, if yuh was kept in a box in Arizona for three years. Whatcha suppose anybody's tryin' to kill off Legg for ? "

" I didn't know they was."

" Somebody shot at him the other night, didn't they ? And Goode says that shot was fired at him to-day."

" He ought to go away," said Scotty, looking gloomily at his cigar, which seemed to be trying to expand into a rose, or a cabbage.

He flung it in a cuspidor, and smoothed his huge moustache.

" We never had no trouble around here until he came," said Scotty. " He's a hoo-doo, that tenderfoot ! "

" How's that dog comin' along, Scotty ? "

" First class. It bit me once, and Al Porter twice."

" Ha, ha, ha, ha ! Don't like officers, eh ? "

" Takes after his owner, I reckon. Gimme somethin' to take the taste of that cigar out of my mouth."

The sheriff drank a glass of liquor and scowled at Plenty Goode, who still sat on the bar-rail, snoring blissfully.

" Don't wake him up," pleaded the bartender. " When that jigger gets on one subject, he never knows when to quit."

" I ain't goin' to wake him up," wearily. " I suppose I'd better go out to the Double Bar 8 and

Investigate that shooting. It won't do no good, though. I've got more prisoners now than I know what to do with. Three of 'em—and a dog ! I wish I wasn't the sheriff."

" Well, cheer up, Scotty ; somebody will prob'ly kill yuh very soon, and then yore troubles will all be over."

" I s'pose that's true."

The sheriff went back to his office, where he found Porter cleaning a Winchester.

" Hear anythin' new ? " growled Porter.

" No. Reckon there's any use investigatin' that shootin' at the Taylor ranch ? "

Porter inserted a piece of white paper in the breech of the rifle and squinted down the barrel.

" With two of the smartest detectives already there ? " he replied. " You'd find out a lot, wouldn't yuh ? "

" Mebbe that's right. I understand they're hired by Le Moyne, or by the Santa Rita mine."

" Mm-m-m-m-m." Porter reached for the oil-can and proceeded to lubricate the mechanism.

" I dunno how a detective can ever find out who held up that train, if he spends all his time runnin' a ranch," said the sheriff.

" Not bein' a detective, I don't know," said Porter coldly. " And what's a lot more, I don't care a —— ! "

CHAPTER XII

JIMMY TAKES A SHOT

FOR the next three days nothing startling happened at the Double Bar 8, except that Jimmy Legg laboured hard with the intricacies of a rope, which invariably tangled around his legs, and a six-shooter, which seemed to ignore the target entirely.

Hashknife and Sleepy humped against the patio wall, absorbing many cigarettes, while they solemnly gave advice to Jimmy, and marvelled that any man could shoot away so much ammunition and never hit anything.

But Jimmy was persistent. He banged away merrily, satisfied if his bullet came within two feet of a tomato-can, at twenty feet, trying to follow Hashknife's advice to shoot low. Apollo, the burro, entirely recovered from his creasing, humped back in the shade of the patio wall, and watched Jimmy with solemn dignity, jerking his one good ear convulsively at each report of the heavy Colt.

Nanah had watched with interest from the door of the ranch-house, until a misdirected bullet smashed through a window near her, after which she lost interest in Jimmy's marksmanship.

Hashknife and Sleepy rounded up several head

of Double Bar 8 horses, getting Marion's opinion on them as a remuda for the coming round-up, and also trying them out. As a result, both of the cowboys were stiff and sore from the unaccustomed shaking which is usually meted out to a rider by horses which have not been ridden for months. Jimmy Legg had tried one, and then retired to the liniment bottle.

Marion decided to ride to Blue Wells, and Jimmy immediately offered to ride with her. Jimmy had not been away from the ranch since the mysterious bullet had nearly robbed him of an ear, and he was anxious to go to town. Regardless of the fact that his torn scalp had not been dressed by a doctor, it was doing very nicely, and he was able to do away with the bandage.

He and Marion did not indulge in much conversation on the way to Blue Wells, because of the fact that most of Jimmy's time was occupied in handling his mount.

" This is rather embarrassing," he told Marion. " I start to say something to you, when this fool horse goes off across the country. I'd rather be thrown off than to have my conversation interrupted every time."

" But you're learning," declared Marion.

" I hope so," dubiously.

" Jimmy, does it mean so much to you—to be a cowboy ? "

Jimmy reined his horse back into the road, clutched his hat just in time to save it, and nodded violently.

" You bet ! Say, it means an awful lot to me, Marion. Darn it, the more I think about it, the more it means."

Marion did not question him any further as they rode down the main street of Blue Wells. Marion dismounted at the sheriff's office, but Jimmy rode on to the Oasis hitch-rack, where he had seen several AK horses tied.

At the Oasis bar he found Johnny Grant, Eskimo Swensen, Oyster Shell, and Tex Alden. Johnny fell upon him with a war-whoop of joy and dragged him to the bar, while Eskimo and Oyster pounded him on the shoulders and examined his scalp, much in the way of a pair of monkeys, gibbering the while.

Tex turned away without speaking and walked outside, while the AK gang leaned Johnny against the bar and demanded loudly of the bartender that he work fast. They questioned Jimmy about the shooting at the Double Bar 8, and his progress as a cowpuncher. In fact, the questions came too fast for Jimmy to answer. But after the second drink he managed to catch his breath, and told them some of the happenings. But he would not drink any more.

" I've got to ride back to the ranch," he told them solemnly. " I brought Miss Taylor to town, and she is down at the jail, visiting with her folks."

The two drinks had made Jimmy rather expansive, and he told them about his roping and shooting lessons ; which caused the AK boys to double up with mirth.

" We was goin' to stop at yore place on the way back," said Johnny Grant. " Bonnette said to tell Miss Taylor that her outfit can use from our wagons. There's plenty of room for all the bed-rolls, and three extra men ain't going to kill off our cook."

" Well, that certainly is thoughtful of him," said Jimmy. " I know Miss Taylor will appreciate it."

" Aw, you better have one more drink," urged Eskimo. " One more won't hurt yuh none."

" Well," Jimmy smiled expansively, " I suppose not. But I'll buy this one."

All of which was acceptable, as it had been long enough since pay-day to find the AK boys in financial straits. They drank a health to Jimmy, and all walked outside. The main street of Blue Wells drowsed in the afternoon sun. A few men humped in shady spots, whittling, discussing nothing much in particular. Even the horses at the hitch-racks drowsed.

Suddenly a commotion started at the sheriff's office. It was not a big commotion, but plainly audible on the silent street. A yellowish-red dog darted out of the office door, whirled around once, as if to get its bearings, and trotted up the street, looking back.

Out of the door came Al Porter. He had a heavy dish in his right hand. Only for a moment did he hesitate, and then started toward the dog, running stiffly, swearing. The dog was Geronimo, the Exhibit A, in the case of the State of Arizona versus the Taylor Outfit.

Running as fast as he was capable, Porter hurled the dish at the dog. But his aim was very faulty, which was attested to by a splintering of window-glass from the front of Louie Sing's restaurant.

The AK gang whooped with mirth. Jimmy Legg, forgetting that ownership of Geronimo might cause complications, ran across the street toward Porter, yelling at him to let the dog alone. Geronimo stopped in an angle between the end of a bench and the wall of Moon's store, and anxiously watched Porter, who had picked up several rocks about the size of eggs, and was preparing to bombard the dog.

Jimmy's three drinks had made him reckless.

"You let that dog alone!" yelped Jimmy.

He was about twenty feet away from the swearing, perspiring Porter, who paused long enough to con-sign Jimmy to a place which was even more arid than Death Valley.

"I'll learn that dog to bite me!" he roared. "I'll smash in his —— skull!"

The first rock struck the end of the bench and glanced into Geronimo, who yelped more from fright than actual distress.

"Stop that, you dirty coyote!" yelled Jimmy.

Porter let fly with another rock, which narrowly missed breaking one of the store windows, and whirled angrily toward Jimmy.

"Who's a coyote?" he snorted.

His right hand swung back to the butt of his gun. It is barely possible that Jimmy's three drinks had ruined his perspective, because he whipped out his gun and shot at Porter, almost before his hand swung away from his hip.

The enraged deputy was off balance, unprepared, his right foot lifted, as he had been following the swing of his throwing arm. And at the crack of Jimmy's gun, his feet seemed to jerk from under him and he came down in the hard street with a crash.

Jimmy stood there in the street, dangling the gun in his hand, while Porter sprawled on his back, his knees jerking. The dog came running toward Jimmy, barking joyfully, and almost knocked Jimmy down.

" Good ——, go away ! " panted Jimmy. " Gug-go away ! "

The three boys from the AK ran past Jimmy, going straight to Porter. The sheriff and Marion were coming from the office, while it seemed to Jimmy that the rest of the world spewed out of every doorway. Then he lost his nerve. Whirling on his heel, he ran to the hitch-rack, mounted his horse and went flailing off down the street, followed by Geronimo, barking wildly.

Porter got slowly to his feet, holding one hand against his head, his face a mixture of anger and wonderment.

" Where'd he hit yuh ? "

" What was the matter ? "

" Who shot yuh ? "

Questions were fired at Porter, who groaned dismally and shoved the anxious sheriff away.

" That —— fool ! " quavered Porter. " Who'd ever think he'd shoot ? I was plumb off balance

—kinda on one heel—and his bullet—take a look at it."

Porter held up his foot and they beheld the reason for the deputy's sudden drop. The heavy bullet had smashed into the high heel, almost into the counter, and the impact had knocked Porter's sole prop from under him. And Porter had hit his head a resounding whack against the ground, which accounted for the fact that Porter stayed down a while.

" And he stole the dog ! " exclaimed the sheriff.

" The dog stole him," amended Johnny Grant.

" I hope he keeps him ! " groaned Porter.   " I'm all through with that dog, evidence or no evidence."

" But we've got to have that dog, Al," insisted the sheriff.   " That's our main evidence."

" Then you get him and do the feedin'.   I never hired out as a menagerie keeper.   He bit me on the wrist, and when I kicked at him, he bit me on the ankle and got loose."

Tex Alden was one of those who had come from Moon's store, and now he spoke to the sheriff :—

" Just why did that dog pull out with Legg ? "

" Why, I dunno, Tex," admitted the sheriff.

" Why did Legg defend the dog ? "

The sheriff looked blankly around.

" I dunno that either, Tex."

" All right."   Tex smiled crookedly and shrugged his shoulders.   He looked at Marion, but did not speak, and turned away.

" What'll yuh do to that kid, Al ? " asked one of the men.

" Do to him ? "   Porter took it under advise-
ment.   " I dunno.   He might 'a' been right.   I
was so mad that I dunno just how things was "

" You reached back for a gun," reminded Eskimo,
and the other three AK cowboys nodded in con-
firmation.

" Yuh did, Al," said Johnny.

" All right," nodded Porter.   " Mebbe I did."

" And the kid thought yuh was goin' to draw
on him," offered Oyster Shell.

" Well, what's all the argument about ? " snarled
the deputy.   " I'll admit he was right.   But,"
Porter mustered a smile, " I hope that dog bites
him when he gits off that horse."

All of which ended all arguments as far as the
guilt or innocence of Jimmy Legg was concerned—
although Jimmy Legg, running his horse back
toward the Double Bar 8, considered himself a
deep-dyed killer.

He imagined that a posse was already on his
trail, and once he saw Geronimo far back in the
road, just topping a rise, and his imagination con-
jured up a dozen armed men, hot on his trail.   The
shooting had made him cold sober, but the taste
of liquor was still on his palate.

His future was indefinite, because his thoughts
ran in circles.   He could see the big deputy, lying
flat in the street, his knees jerking.   Everything
else was blotted out by that picture.   He tried to
remember just why he had fired the shot, but it
was like a half-forgotten dream—something that
had happened long ago.

His horse was plastered with lather when he rode in at the patio gate and dismounted near the well. Hashknife and Sleepy were just coming from the ranch-house door, realising from the condition of the horse that something was wrong.

"What's wrong, Jimmy?" asked Hashknife.

Jimmy flapped his arms weakly, and there was a decided catch in his throat.

"I just killed the deputy sheriff," he said.

Hashknife stepped closer and grasped Jimmy by a shoulder.

"You done what?"

Jimmy gulped and nodded.

"Ye-yes, I did. I—I——"

"Take it easy, kid," said Hashknife. "Set down here on the curb and tell us about it."

"I can't." Jimmy shook his head nervously. "I've got to keep going. They're after me, don't you see?"

"All right, kid. If they're after you, this is a fine place for 'em to get you."

"But I can't stay here, Hashknife."

"Sure yuh can, Jimmy. Let's talk it over. Runnin' away won't help yuh none. You'd lose out."

Geronimo came into the patio, dust-covered, his tongue hanging out, tail wagging. Jimmy had set a hot pace from town, but the dog had found him. He sat down on his haunches in front of Jimmy and put a paw on Jimmy's knee.

"Where'd the dog come from?" asked Sleepy.

Jimmy looked at Geronimo, and Geronimo looked at Jimmy.

" He is my dog," said Jimmy slowly. " It's the dog they had in jail—the evidence against Taylor."

" Your dog, Jimmy ? " asked Hashknife.

" Oh, yes," Jimmy nodded slowly. " You see, I was afraid to tell anybody."

" All right," said Hashknife. " Now, tell us about the killin' of the deputy sheriff, Jimmy."

And Jimmy told them, while the two cowboys asked a question here and there to clarify things somewhat.

" Well, it looks to me as if it was a case of self-defence," said Hashknife, when Jimmy had finished his story.

" He really reached for his gun," said Jimmy. " I realised it."

" What I'd like to know is, how in —— did yuh ever hit him ? " queried Sleepy.

" I—I suppose it was because he's larger than a tin can."

" Where do yuh reckon yuh hit him ? "

" Oh, I don't know," wailed Jimmy. " It must have been through the heart, because he fell down so quickly—and his knees were jerking."

" That's good shootin' for the first time," said Sleepy dryly. " Where is Marion ? "

" Oh, I forgot her ! I must have been excited."

" You prob'ly would be," agreed Hashknife. " What I want you to do right now is to tell me all, about ownin' this dog."

" Oh, yes, about the dog." Jimmy jerked

nervously at the sound of a noise outside the patio gate, but it was only Apollo, rubbing his shoulder against the wall.

Jimmy sighed deeply.

" I suppose that was a dirty trick. But when I found out that—that the dog was supposed to belong to a robber, I was afraid to claim him. He ran away from me that night in Blue Wells, you see."

And then James Eaton Legg went ahead and told them about his experience with the express messenger. Hashknife grinned, when Jimmy told of that battle in the express car, and of how the messenger had described him as being a big, burly man, who tried to draw a gun.

" His lyin' saves you a lot of trouble," said Hashknife, when Jimmy had finished his tale. " He didn't want anybody to think he had been whipped by a smaller man."

" I suppose so ; but I'll go to town and tell 'em that the dog belongs to me. I might as well shoulder it all now."

" I wish yuh wouldn't," said Hashknife. " Let things ride as they are for a while. If they arrest yuh for shootin' the deputy, mebbe yuh can make a self-defence out of it. Yuh say that the AK boys saw it ? They'll prob'ly alibi yuh, 'cause they don't like the sheriff. Under the circumstances a man could lie a little and not bend his conscience too much."

" Yuh should have stayed and seen the finish," said Sleepy. " It would 'a' looked better."

" I know it." Jimmy sighed wearily. " But all I could think about was to run away. I've never killed a man before."

" Prob'ly the first time he ever was killed, too."

" Oh, don't joke about it ! It's a terrible thing."

" Pshaw, I wasn't jokin', Jimmy."

" I know, but——"

A horse swung in through the patio gate, and Jimmy almost fell off the curb ; but it was only Marion. She looked at Jimmy and began laughing. Geronimo barked joyfully and tried to jump up to her stirrup.

But Jimmy only stared at her blankly, his mouth open.

" What's the joke ? " asked Hashknife seriously.

" Dud-don't laugh," pleaded Jimmy. " It isn't anything to laugh about."

Between chuckles of merriment Marion managed to tell them what Jimmy had done, while Jimmy, his eyes and mouth wide open, leaned against the curb, gasping like a fish out of water.

Marion described how Jimmy had ridden out of Blue Wells, followed by the dog, and Sleepy cried against the shoulder of her horse. But Jimmy was too relieved to laugh.

" Well," he said solemnly, " I guess I'll have to pick something bigger than a man next time. Really, there should be something big enough for me to hit."

" You ought to attack a fort," laughed Sleepy.

They unsaddled Marion's horse, while Jimmy took care of his own exhausted mount. He was so happy that he tried to take the saddle off without uncinching it.

" I expect the sheriff will be out here soon," Marion told them. " He wants that dog. It bit Al Porter twice to-day, but they've got to keep it for evidence."

" They don't know it's here," said Hashknife. " Let's hide it."

" Hide it ? But that wouldn't be lawful."

" It isn't lawful to hold yore folks on that kind of evidence either. Where can we put the dog ? "

" In the cellar," suggested Sleepy. " The one beneath the kitchen."

" But won't they search ? "

" Prob'ly. Put a rug over the trap-door, and they'll never see it."

It did not take them long to dump Geronimo into the cellar, where Sleepy made him a good bed and put in a bucket of water. The dog accepted his new quarters without any protest, and Nanah grinned when she put an old rug over the trap-door, and moved over a table to rest on it.

The three men were in the bunk-house when the sheriff showed up, about thirty minutes later. He looked around the patio, expecting to see the dog, and dismounted. Hashknife shook hands with him. Jimmy did not put in an appearance.

" You heard what happened in town, didn't yuh ? " asked the sheriff. Hashknife agreed that he had.

" It ended all right," remarked the sheriff.

" Except that the main exhibit of the Taylor case followed Legg out of town."

" What exhibit was that ? "

" The dog. Legg came here, didn't he ? "

" Oh, yeah. But I don't know anythin' about the dog. Jimmy said the trouble started over a dog, and Miss Taylor said the dog followed Jimmy out of Blue Wells, but it prob'ly went back."

" Yea-a-a-ah ? Went back—where ? "

" Why, to Blue Wells."

" I don't think so, Hartley."

" Didja search the town ? "

The sheriff, of course, hadn't. He had taken it for granted that the dog followed Legg all the way to the Double Bar 8, and upon sober reflection on his part it was reasonable to suppose that the dog had stopped and turned back to town.

" The kid was kinda scared, wasn't he ? " asked the sheriff.

" Naturally would be," grinned Hashknife. " He thought he had killed Porter."

" I dunno how he ever missed hittin' Al some'ers beside in the heel. They wasn't twenty feet apart. That derned tenderfoot is goin' to kill somebody before he gits through. He's comin' closer every time. By golly, I dodge every time I see him. He's such a bad shot that he worries me."

As they were laughing over Jimmy's marksmanship, Lee Barnhardt rode in on his sway-backed mount and dismounted beside them.

" You rode too fast for me," he told the sheriff.

" I saw you start out, but you didn't stop when I yelled."

" I didn't hear yuh, Lee."

Marion came from the house, and Barnhardt took some mail from his pocket, which he gave to her.

" The postmaster said you forgot to get it," he said. " I was coming out ; so I brought it."

The mail consisted of a few circulars and a weekly newspaper.

" I asked for mail for you, boys," Barnhardt told Hashknife.

" We're not likely to get any," smiled Hashknife. " Thank yuh just the same."

Barnhardt turned to the sheriff.

" What about that dog ? "

" Not here.   Mebbe it never left town, Lee. Yo're not worryin', are yuh ? "

" Not me.   I'd be just as well satisfied if it never came back."

" That's what I thought.   Are yuh ready to ride back ? "

The lawyer shook his head.

" I'm in no hurry, Scotty."

" Well, I am. So long, folks."

Jimmy ventured out after the sheriff had gone, and wanted to know everything the sheriff had said.   He was so glad to know that the law was not on his trail that he even spoke pleasantly to Lee Barnhardt.

Marion went in the house, and Sleepy sat down in the shade with Jimmy, leaving Hashknife with the lawyer.

" Naturally, we are both working in the interests
of the Taylor family," said the lawyer confidentially.
" Now, I'd like to know what progress you have
made in your observations."

Hashknife looked at him keenly.

" I don't reckon I understand yuh, Barnhardt."

" No ? "   Barnhardt smiled knowingly.   " For
your own information I will say that Chet Le Moyne
admitted your connections with the Santa Rita
mining company."

" He did, eh ? "   Hashknife was wearing his
poker face now.

" Yes.   It is rather difficult to keep a thing like
that from becoming common knowledge.   Folks
naturally wondered what your business might be."

" I suppose," seriously.   " But I don't reckon it
makes much difference, does it ? "

" Oh, no.   I have not mentioned it to any one ;
but I was curious to know what you had found out,
because I am anxious for any new development
which will serve my clients."

" Well, I can't tell yuh much.   In fact, I can't
tell yuh anythin'."

" Anything you told me would be in strictest
confidence."

" Yeah, I realise that."

But although the Blue Wells lawyer waited
patiently, the tall cowboy remained silent.   Then—

" Just an inkling of what you are doing would
serve to cheer up my clients."

Hashknife shifted his position and looked Barnhardt squarely in the eye.   The level stare of the

cold-eyed cowboy caused Barnhardt's gaze to shift. He had the uncomfortable feeling that Hashknife could read his mind.

" Barnhardt," said Hashknife earnestly, " do you think I'm a —— fool ? "

" Oh, no ; not at all. Well," Barnhardt turned away, " I suppose I may as well go back. No hard feelings, I hope. Being in charge of the Taylor defence, I would naturally be interested in any new developments in the case."

Barnhardt mounted his sway-backed horse and rode away, his elbows flapping, his trouser-legs crawling up. About a mile from the Double Bar 8 he drew rein and let his horse walk slowly along the dusty road, while he took an envelope from his pocket. The flap had already been torn loose. He drew out the letter and perused it closely. The envelope, postmarked Chicago, was addressed to H. Hartley, Blue Wells, Arizona, and the letter read :—

DEAR SIR,—A wire from us to James Eaton Legg, San Francisco, California, brought a reply from his former place of residence to the effect that Mr. Legg had left there and had left his forwarding address as Blue Wells, Arizona. This may be a coincidence, or it may be because of some former information. Trusting that you will be able to furnish us with valuable information soon, we beg to remain,

" Sincerely yours,
" LEESOM & BRAND."

Barnhardt's lips were shut tightly and the muscles of his jaw bulged as he tore the letter into tiny fragments, swung his horse off the road, and scattered the bits of paper into a mesquite tangle. He turned in his saddle and looked back toward the Double Bar 8, as he reined his horse back to the road.

"Hashknife Hartley," he said earnestly, "do you think I'm a —— fool?"

But whether Hashknife did, or didn't—Barnhardt had no way of knowing. He could only guess, and possibly he guessed wrong. At any rate he rode back to Blue Wells in a black frame of mind, and the first man he met was Chet Le Moyne.

"I've just been out to the Double Bar 8," he told Le Moyne. "And I had a talk with your detectives."

"You did, eh. What did they tell you?"

"That would be telling, Chet. I told them I knew they were working for the Santa Rita."

"Yeah?" coldly. "And then?"

"Oh, they didn't deny it. But I don't think they've found out very much."

"Possibly not."

Le Moyne watched Barnhardt ride down to his office, tie his horse, and go inside. The face of the handsome paymaster twisted angrily as his gloomy eyes squinted against the sun.

"I wonder if Barnhardt is just a plain fool, or——"

Le Moyne shook his head and went on his way.

. . . . . .

That evening Hashknife, Sleepy, and Jimmy

rode to Blue Wells. There were few people in town, and while Jimmy and Sleepy played pool at the Oasis saloon, Hashknife found the sheriff at his office. The sheriff was pleasant and curious, especially when Hashknife talked over with him the evidence in the Taylor case.

The subject of the AK boys' locking the sheriff in his own cell came up, and the sheriff explained that the reason no one discovered his plight was because Al Porter, the deputy, was at Encinas, visiting a girl, and did not get back until morning.

" Does that Santa Rita pay-roll come in at the same time every month ? " asked Hashknife.

" I dunno."

" They say that the paymaster always takes the money from here to the mine."

" I reckon he does."

" And somebody would have to know it was comin' that day."

" Oh, they must 'a' knowed about it, Hartley."

" How would Taylor have found it out ? "

" That's hard to say. Chet Le Moyne, the paymaster, is kinda sweet on Miss Taylor, and——"

" And he might have told her, eh ? "

" I don't say he did, Hartley."

" But for the sake of an argument, it could 'a' happened. She might 'a' mentioned the fact that Chet was comin' in to get the pay-roll, eh ? Is that what yuh was thinkin' ? "

" Mebbe." The sheriff did not want to commit himself.

" And this Le Moyne was at the depot to get the pay-roll ? "

" Yeah. He was here earlier in the evenin', and somebody said he went out to see Miss Taylor."

" But he was at the depot to get the money, was he ? "

" Yeah."

" And you think there was four men in on the deal ? "

" Sure. The fourth one got on at Encinas. It was his job to put the messenger out of commission, I reckon."

" This happened out where the AK road turns off the Encinas road, near the railroad track, I understand. They cut the express car loose from the rest of the train, ran it up there, blew the safe, and got the money. The engine crew say they had sort of a battle with 'em, after they left the car. Then the engine crew ran the engine and express car back to where they had cut loose from the rest of the train, picked it up, and came on to Blue Wells. Is that it ? "

" Yeah, that's what happened."

" This express messenger and the man who got on the car at Encinas fought in the car, but finally fell out. Do yuh know if this was before or after the train was cut in two ? "

The sheriff cogitated deeply.

" I never did hear, but—say, it must 'a' been after the train was broken, because they picked up the messenger on their way to here. Yessir, it must 'a' been after they cut off the express car, because that messenger sure was picked up. He never walked to the train."

" The messenger described the man who fought him, didn't he ? "

" Well, he said it was a big, husky sort of a feller. I don't think there's any question about him bein' one of the gang. He used that dog as a reason for gettin' on that car."

" Then why did he walk to the scene of the robbery, take the dog from the express car and disappear ? "

" Prob'ly scared that some one would recognise the dog."

" The messenger and engine crew had already seen it. If it belonged to Taylor, do yuh reckon they'd take the dog back to their ranch, where any one could find it ? "

The sheriff twisted his moustache thoughtfully. This was something he had not thought about.

" Anybody would recognise that dog," said Hashknife.

" Yore argument sounds pretty good," admitted the sheriff. " But it don't make much difference, because we can't find that dog. Al Porter is glad, I suppose. The darn thing hates him. Bit him every time it had a chance. Growls every time he shows up."

" You'll have to find the dog before the trial, won't yuh ? "

" I s'pose the prosecutin' attorney will raise —— if it ain't here. Still, it's been identified ; so that prob'ly won't make a lot of difference."

" What became of Wade, the railroad detective ? "

" Oh, he went back. Yuh see, he decided that Taylor was guilty ; so there wasn't anythin' more for him to do here."

Hashknife went back to the saloon, and they made it a three-handed game of pool. It was about nine o'clock when they decided to go back to the ranch, as there was no excitement at all in Blue Wells. The moonlight was so bright that, following Hashknife's suggestion, they rode in single file about fifty feet apart.

That shot from the hills had made Hashknife cautious, and he knew that three riders, bunched, would make an easy target in that moonlight. But their return was uneventful, except that there were no lights in the windows of the ranch-house.

" That sure looks all wrong," declared Hashknife.

" Mebbe not," said Sleepy. " Marion and Nanah might be enjoyin' the moonlight."

" They might, but we'll play safe by thinkin' they're not."

The three men dismounted a hundred yards from the house and went cautiously to the patio gate. There was not a sound. The rear of the ranch-house flung a long shadow across the patio. Hashknife watched and listened for a while, and then strode boldly inside. A door creaked, and they heard Marion's voice :—

" Is that you, Hashknife ? " she spoke softly.

" It sure is," replied Hashknife. " What's the matter ? "

" Come here."

They went softly across the patio and up to the door, where she let them in. They could see the silhouette of Nanah against a window, where she was watching. Marion closed the door softly.

" There wasn't any light," said Hashknife.

" Nanah saw you leave your horses," said Marion. " She knew who it was. About half an hour ago Nanah and I were sitting on the back porch in the moonlight. It was wonderful out there, but it was getting cool ; so we came in. There were no lamps lighted.

" And Nanah swears she saw a man looking in the window, where she is now. I told her she must be seeing things, but she persisted. So we did not light a lamp. We watched and watched, but the man did not come back. I went to the rear door and opened it a little. It squeaks a little, you know. Then I saw a man cross the patio. He was all humped up, and it seemed to me as though he had been looking in the window of the bunk-house. I can't be sure about it. I'm sure he did not suspect that I had seen him, because he stopped in the gateway for quite a while. Then he stepped into the shadow on the other side of the wall."

" How long ago was this ? " asked Hashknife.

" Not over thirty minutes ago."

" He must have been lookin' for us," grinned Sleepy.

" And if he seen us sneak in here he'll know we're on to him," said Hashknife. " But we've got to take a chance. Come out on the porch. Tell Nanah to light the lamps."

The old Indian woman bustled around, lighting lamps, while the rest of them followed Hashknife to the rear porch.

" I'll go first," whispered Hashknife. " One man only makes one target. If the coast is clear, I'll whistle a tune, and Sleepy, you, and Jimmy come over there."

Hashknife kept well in the shadow in crossing the patio, and in a minute or two he began whistling. Sleepy and Jimmy crossed to the bunk-house, where the door was open. Hashknife lighted the lamp, which was on a table about midway of the room.

Then he motioned Sleepy and Jimmy back to the doorway, where he followed them out, closing the door.

" Duck down as low as yuh can and sneak back to the house," he whispered. They got back to the house and crept silently in.

Hashknife stepped in close to a rear window, where he could get a clear view of the patio, and watched through a break in the curtain.

" If he didn't see our horses, he'll think we're in the bunk-house," said Hashknife. " If he seen us leave our horses and do an Injun sneak, he'll know we're on to him, and prob'ly fog away from here."

" Do you think it's the man who has been trying to kill me ? " asked Jimmy.

" Might be."

Suddenly Hashknife jerked back. A blinding flash filled the room, followed by a terrific jarring crash, which fairly threw them off their feet. The lamp was extinguished ; pictures fell from the walls, and a moment later the house seemed to be bombarded with missiles from every angle.

Hashknife had fallen back against a table, but now he got to his feet, groping in the dark. Sleepy was swearing dazedly. Dust and smoke eddied in through the broken windows, and with it was the odour of dynamite; the unmistakable scent of nitro-glycerine.

" Is anybody hurt ? " gasped Hashknife, scratching a match and holding it above his head. Nanah was sitting against the wall, her eyes goggling out of an impassive face. Marion had got to her feet and was reaching for something to steady herself with, while Jimmy had backed against the wall, his arms outspread against it, his feet braced.

" What was it ? " whispered Marion, staring wide-eyed at Hashknife.

" Somebody dynamited us, I reckon." He strode to the door and flung it open, while the others crowded close behind him. Where once had stood the adobe bunk-house, there was only a pile of adobe bricks, twisted timbers. The patio was a mass of adobe. On the porch of the ranch-house was the splintered door, torn from its hinges and flung across the patio.

Hashknife ran across the yard, vaulted across the debris, and went out through a gaping hole in the patio wall, heading for the stables. Through some freak of dynamite explosion, the force seemed to have been in the opposite direction to the stables, with the result that none of the stock was injured, and the stable still intact.

It did not take Hashknife long to find that nothing had been injured in the stable. A decidedly feminine shriek from the patio sent him running back through the broken wall, where he almost ran into Apollo, the ancient burro.

" He was under that pile of stuff," yelled Sleepy. " Rised up like a darned ghost and almost scared Marion to death."

Marion was laughing foolishly, almost hysterically.

" —— good thing I see man," declared Nanah solemnly.

" You bet it was l " agreed Hashknife warmly. " If yuh didn't see that man, we'd be in bad shape now, Nanah. Good gosh ! Can yuh imagine what would 'a' happened to us, if we'd 'a' been in that bunk-house ? "

" Yeah, and we'd better look a little out," said Sleepy nervously. " The little side-winder that touched off that blast will prob'ly want to see if he done a good job."

" He'll not come back to-night, Sleepy. He's high-tailin' it out of this section right now. I'll betcha yuh could hear that explosion in Blue Wells."

Marion shivered in the cold breeze, as she looked at the moonlit wreck.

" Oh, what will happen next ? " she wondered aloud.

" Somebody," said Hashknife, " is goin' to hear the echo of that blast, and it sure is goin' to ache his ears."

They tried to find their bed-rolls, but the outer wall of the bunk-house, which was about two feet thick of adobe, had fallen in on the floor, and it would require much digging to get down even to the bunk levels.

They went after their horses and put them in the stable, after which they borrowed a few blankets from Marion. Jimmy insisted that he be allowed to stand guard with them, but Hashknife decreed that Jimmy sleep in the house, while Sleepy rolled in his blankets at the hay-mow window of the stable, which, since the bunk-house was no more, gave him a fair view of the patio and rear of the house. Hashknife went out about a hundred feet from the front of the house, and coiled up in his blankets in the cover of a mesquite, where he could watch the front of the ranch-house. But nothing came, except the cold, gray dawn, which was a long time coming.

There was an exodus from Blue Wells, when the news of the dynamiting reached there, and the Double Bar 8 held a great gathering of the cattle-clan, who came to view the ruins and to give an opinion. Some of them seemed to think that perhaps Apostle Paul Taylor had had some dynamite stored in the bunk-house, and that it had exploded.

Tex Alden came and viewed the ruins with gloomy eyes ; Barnhardt perched on a pile of adobe and crumbled the clay between his fingers, and looked wise. The sheriff talked to every one who seemed to have any kind of a theory—and knew no more about it than he did when he came.

The women grouped around Marion, and " Oh'd " and " Ah'd," like a lot of old hens clucking over a sudden fright. Hashknife said nothing, but listened much. Le Moyne came to him and tried to find out what Hashknife thought about it, but went away with the feeling that this tall cowboy knew less than any of them.

With Le Moyne was Dug Haley, who quarrelled loudly with Al Porter over what dynamite would or would not do. Sleepy Stevens horned into the argument with a dissertation on " the dynamic principles of combustion," in which he used the words " epiglottis," " atomiser," and " dogmatic " numberless times ; much to the confusion of Al Porter, who was forced to admit that all he knew about dynamite was that " the —— stuff busts and raises ——."

It was not often that Antelope Neal, owner of the Oasis, went out of Blue Wells, but he did ride down to see what had happened to the Double Bar 8. Neal was a small, gray-haired man, who seldom had anything to say. He was a square gambler, and was respected as such in Blue Wells.

Hashknife noticed that Tex Alden and Antelope Neal stood apart from the crowd for quite a while, talking confidentially, eyeing him at times, and causing Hashknife to suspect that he was the subject of their conversation.

When the crowd began to thin out, it seemed that Tex tried to start a conversation with Marion, but she evidently preferred the attention of Jimmy Legg, and Tex retired, his lips set in a thin line, his eyes hard and speculative.

Lee Barnhardt noticed that Marion had evaded

Tex, and it seemed to amuse the Blue Wells attorney. He sidled in beside Tex, who paid no attention to him.

" Tex, you're not going to let a tenderfoot tramp cut you out, are you ? " he asked, possibly trying to be sympathetic.

Tex's action was almost as sudden as dynamite. He hooked his right fist against Barnhardt's jaw, knocking him almost through the patio gate. Needless to say, Barnhardt stayed down. Tex stepped over to him, glanced down, turned to the crowd and studied them coldly. Then, without a word, he walked to his horse, mounted and rode away.

Several men ran to Barnhardt and tried to help him to his feet ; but standing up was one thing that Barnhardt did not care about in the least. He sagged weakly, goggle-eyed.

" As cool as a cow-cumber," said Al Porter.

" Cucumber," corrected Dug Haley.

" I said what I meant ! " snapped Porter. " If you wants to correct me on vegetation, you better mean the same thing that I do."

" There's been enough fightin'," observed the sheriff. " Did anybody hear what caused Tex to hit Barnhardt ? "

Nobody had. Some one secured a bucket of water, which they sluiced over the helpless Barnhardt. It made a mess of him, but served to jolt him back to consciousness. After a minute or two he was able to stand on his feet, but his jaw did not function properly. Hashknife examined it but found it was not broken.

" Why did he hit yuh, Lee ? " asked the sheriff.

" Idnuk," said Lee painfully. Interpreted, this might be construed to mean, " I don't know."

And this was all the explanation he was willing to mumble. He went out to his sway-backed horse, and headed for Blue Wells, riding slowly and caressing his jaw.

The sheriff was the last to leave, and he would have stayed longer, except that the four cowboys from the AK ranch rode in. They had heard of the dynamiting in Blue Wells. The sheriff did not care for their company ; so he rode away.

" That shore is another wreck of the Hesperus, ain't she ? " said Eskimo Swensen. " Wham ! I'll betcha she made some noise."

" It came near being serious," said Jimmy.

Johnny Grant grinned widely and slapped Jimmy on the back.

" You derned hoodoo ! It looks as though this was the third time they'd tried to kill yuh off. I dunno what they'll use next."

" Tie him on a railroad track," suggested Oyster.

Johnny drew Hashknife aside, and they sat down together on a pile of shattered adobe bricks.

" I've been wantin' to talk with you, Hartley," said Johnny seriously. " Yo're workin' on this hold-up case, ain't yuh ? "

" Well ? " Hashknife admitted nothing.

" I heard yuh was ; so I'm goin' to tell yuh what I know about it."

And while the other boys examined the wreckage, Johnny Grant told Hashknife of that night in Blue

Wells, when they got drunk and locked the sheriff in his own cell. And of the incident at the train, when they staged an impromptu battle with the engineer and fireman ; not knowing what it was all about.

He told Hashknife of the man who came along the track in the dark, went into the express car, and got the dog.

" Somebody cut our broncs loose that night," said Johnny. " I understand that the sheriff's horses were also turned loose, and it kinda looks as though it was done to prevent a posse from trailin' 'em. If course, they wouldn't know that Al Porter was in Encinas, visitin' his girl, and that the sheriff was in jail."

Hashknife grinned widely and thanked Johnny for his information.

" Thasall right," said Johnny. " Yo're sure welcome. Yuh see, we don't care much for the sheriff and his deputy. They said we ought to be run out of the country ; so we kept still about what happened to us. But when they jailed the Taylor outfit, I just got to thinkin' that mebbe our evidence might help to land the right ones. I didn't want to give it to Wade, the railroad detective, because he acted so smart ; but I'm givin' it to you, because you—because I had a talk with Goode, over at the X Bar 6."

" Well, that may not help us all the way out, but it's somethin' to grab on to," smiled Hashknife. " That feller Goode probably lied a lot about us, but he means all right, I guess."

" Well," confessed Johnny gravely, " he sure scared me into tellin' yuh all I knew."

" You look like a feller that scares easy," grinned Hashknife. " I'll betcha all three of you fellers would run from a shadow."

" Well, yuh can't do much damage to a shadow, yuh know. We'd like yuh to know that if yuh need three fellers that are strong in the muscle and weak in the head, yuh might call on us."

" Thanks, Grant. I reckon Nanah and Marion are cookin' dinner, and if I was you, I'd stick around for the meal. Marion wants to thank yuh for offerin' accommodations to us on the round-up."

" George Bonnette done that, Hartley. 'S funny Tex Alden didn't offer to take care of yuh."

" I reckon he's sore about Jimmy bein' here."

" M-m-m-m-m-m. Hartley, no matter what yore personal opinion is of Tex Alden, he's a white man, and a good cow-hand. Mebbe he's kinda off colour on account of carin' a lot for that girl, but he's a square shooter—all the time."

" Yeah ? He ordered Jimmy Legg to get out of the country. That night Jimmy was shot, just after he had left Marion Taylor, at the front of the Blue Wells hotel. A little later on, a shot from the hill out there almost got him again."

" I know that." Johnny shook his head. " If I was goin' off at half-cock, I'd nod toward Tex, wouldn't you ? "

" I suppose I would, Grant—but I don't."

" No ? Well, that's good. I talked with Tex

the other day. He admits that it looks as if he done it."

Marion called to them from the rear door, and they headed for the wash-bench, dropping the subject of Tex Alden.

And while they ate dinner at the Double Bar 8, Lee Barnhardt rode into Blue Wells, stabled his horse, and went to see the doctor, who did a little to alleviate the pain in his jaw. Back in his office, he filled his pipe and tried to enjoy a smoke, but flung the pipe aside, because he couldn't keep his mind on tobacco. It was the one time in his life that Lee Barnhardt was thoroughly mad. Just now he hated everybody, and everything—especially Tex Alden.

And while his anger was at fever-heat, Scotty Olson, the sheriff, walked into the office.

" How's yore jaw ? " asked the sheriff.

" None of your business ! "

The exclamation seemed to hurt Lee's jaw, and he clapped a hand to the side of his face, shutting one eye tightly.

" I reckon it's all well," said the sheriff sarcastically. " Tex hit yuh a dinger of a punch, didn't he. I never did see a feller flatten out prettier than you did. You was jist about as animated as a scarecrow, after yuh pull the braces out of it. I asked Tex a while ago why he hit yuh, and he said for me to ask you."

" And you came to ask me, did you ? " Barnhardt was almost crying with anger. " You haven't a brain in your head."

" I thought there was a reason," said the sheriff mildly. " Of course, if he was jist doin' it for fun——"

" Fun, eh ? " gritted Barnhardt. " I'll make him think it was fun. He owes the X Bar 6 eight thousand dollars, and he'll pay it, or go to jail for embezzlement. I'll show him ! And for your own information, I'll tell you that Tex knew the money for the Santa Rita was coming in on that train."

" How did he know that, Lee ? "

" I told him it was ! "

" How did you know ? "

" I guessed it."

The sheriff sat down and studied the situation, while the lawyer caressed his sore jaw and wondered if he was showing good judgment in telling all this about Tex.

" And you think Tex held up that train, Lee ? "

" I didn't say that, Scotty."

" No, I know yuh didn't ; but yuh hinted at it. If Tex hears this, he'll hit yuh with somethin' besides his fist."

" I suppose." Lee looked gloomily at the wall, one eye half shut from the pain in his jaw.

Came the sound of a step at the doorway, and Tex Alden came in. Barnhardt jerked up his head quickly, and stared at the man who had knocked him cold.

" Hallo, Scotty," said Tex evenly.

He did not speak to Barnhardt, as he came up to the lawyer's desk, drawing a bulky package from his pocket.

" I owe yuh that much, Barnhardt," Tex said coldly. " Mebbe yuh better count it."

Barnhardt swallowed heavily, but made no move to pick up the money. Tex eyed him for a moment, turned and walked out, without saying anything more. Barnhardt shifted uneasily, but finally picked up the package, walked to his small safe, opened it with a key, and put away the package.

He came back and sat down, making no explanation.

" Tex wasn't very cheerful," observed Scotty.

Barnhardt shook his head and sighed deeply.

" I think I'll take a little trip, Scotty ; kinda get away until time for that trial. I've been pretty steady on the job for two years, and a little change would do me good."

" A change does anybody good," admitted the sheriff. " I'd like to go with yuh. What'll yuh do, close yore office ? "

" I think so. I won't be gone more than a week, but I think, under the circumstances, I should go away until things clear a little."

" I suppose so, Lee."

The sheriff thought it would really be a wise thing for Barnhardt to go away for a while, and he said so to Hashknife that evening, when Hashknife stopped at the office for a few minutes. They were discussing the incident at the Double Bar 8, and Hashknife wondered how Barnhardt's jaw was feeling. The sheriff told of Tex's bringing a package of money to Lee Barnhardt, and he also told

Hashknife what Barnhardt had said about Tex knowing about that shipment of money.

" I wouldn't tell that to anybody else," said the sheriff. " But it appears that you're workin' on the case, and yuh ought to know about these things."

" When does Barnhardt intend to leave ? " asked Hashknife.

" He didn't say ; but I expect he'll leave to-morrow. Between me and you, he's scared of Tex Alden, and he wants to git away for a few days to let Tex cool off. Lee talks too much."

" That's a human failin'," smiled Hashknife.

But Lee Barnhardt did not go on any trip. When he got up the following morning he found that some one had opened his safe during the night, and had looted it of everything it contained. The bank did not have a safety vault ; so Barnhardt found himself cleaned out, as everything he owned was in his own safe.

He sat down at his desk and stared at the empty valise, which he had brought along and placed beside the safe. His clothes were packed in a larger valise. He seemed stunned, his vacant gaze fixed upon the half-open door of the safe.

The fruits of two years' work had been in that safe, when he locked the office the night before. He had never feared a robbery, because a lawyer's safe usually only held papers, of no value to any one except to the lawyer.

His dazed condition passed, leaving him in a state of perspiration. He got to his feet and

staggered over to the safe, peering within, trying
to convince himself that it was only a dream.
He went to the front door and gazed out at the
street. It was fairly early in the morning, and
there were few people in evidence. He heard the
train leave the station ; the train he had intended
leaving on, and he turned away, choking a curse.

He went to his desk, and with shaking fingers
he opened a drawer and took out a revolver, which
he put in his pocket. He unbuttoned his vest,
disclosing a narrow strap across his bosom, attesting
to the fact that he was wearing a shoulder-holster.
Then he sat down, trying to think just what to do.

" I've got to find Tex Alden," he told himself.
" Tex saw me put that money in my safe. ——
him, he paid his debt before a witness, and then
took it back—took everything in the safe. If he
don't give it back to me, I'll kill him."

He flung the two valises behind his desk and
walked to the door. Al Porter was coming toward
the office. Barnhardt tried to appear indifferent,
although he knew Porter would question him. As
Porter neared the office, Marion Taylor, Jimmy
Legg, and Sleepy came riding down the street.
Porter came up to Barnhardt, but did not speak,
and they watched the riders draw up in front of
them.

" Good-morning, Mr. Barnhardt," said Marion.
" We looked for you at the depot a while ago.
Did you decide to not go away ? "

Barnhardt nodded dumbly, because he dared not
speak.

" Where's the tall feller ? " asked Porter.

" He went away on the train," said Sleepy, beginning the manufacture of a cigarette.

" Went away, eh ? Gone to stay ? "

" No-o-o ; just to Encinas."

Barnhardt swallowed heavily and tried to smile.

" That's where Al's girl lives," he offered.

" He may see her," replied Sleepy seriously.

Porter stared at Sleepy, wondering if this innocent-eyed cowboy meant anything by that remark.

" We came in pretty early," said Marion, " and I wonder if the sheriff will let me in the jail."

" He's in the office," growled Porter. " I reckon he will."

They moved on toward the jail, and Porter turned angrily to Barnhardt.

" That was a —— of a remark to make ! You ain't got no interest in my girl, have yuh ? "

" Not a particle."

" Then never mind about her ; *sabe ?* You monkey with my business and you'll get worse than Tex Alden gave yuh."

" Did you come up here to pick a fight ? " queried Barnhardt.

" Any old time I look for trouble, I won't pick out a wide-mouthed lawyer, that's a cinch."

Porter turned on his heel and went to the stable, where he saddled his horse and rode out of town.

Barnhardt waited until the three riders had left the sheriff's office, and then went down there. The sheriff looked quizzically at him.

" I thought you was goin' away this mornin',
Lee."

" Changed my mind," said Barnhardt. " May
go to-morrow."

The sheriff nodded and looked at some papers
on his desk.

" Hartley went away this mornin'," offered
Barnhardt.

The sheriff looked up.

" Yeah, they said he did ; went to Encinas."

" Yes. I guess he expected me to go on the
same train."

" Prob'ly did. I told him yuh was goin' away
this mornin'."

Barnhardt went back to his office, his mind still
travelling in circles. He knew what would happen
if he accused Tex Alden of opening the safe. Tex
was hot-headed, and Barnhardt knew he could never
best Tex in any kind of a fair fight. If he accused
Tex of theft, he'd never get his money and papers
back.

So Barnhardt decided to wait and see, even if
the waiting did gall his soul. No one, except himself and the man who opened the safe, knew that
such a thing had been done. He had thought of
having Tex arrested, but decided that his evidence
against Tex only consisted of Tex's knowing that
the eight thousand was in the safe. Barnhardt had
counted the package of money, when he was alone,
and it contained that amount of currency.

Sleepy, Jimmy, and Marion did not ride back to
the ranch on the road, but circled through the

hills. It was early morning, and they were in no hurry to return. A coyote invited them to a race, and they gave him what he was looking for. Only a barrier of mesquite, into which he sped like a gray shadow, saved him from Sleepy's loop.

Flocks of white-wing doves hurtled past them, heading for the water-holes; quail called from the slopes; a deer broke from a thicket, and after a few short, stiff-legged jumps, headed up a slope, head cocked back, walking jerkily.

They were nearing the ranch when they descried a flock of buzzards, circling low over a little ravine, like scraps of black paper, caught in the grip of a whirlwind.

" Somebody lost a cow," said Sleepy, " and it's eatin' time for Mr. Buzzard."

" I hope it isn't any of our stock," said Marion. " We can't afford to feed any buzzards this year."

Jimmy evinced a desire to investigate; so he and Sleepy rode down to the ravine, while Marion circled higher on the hill. The air suddenly filled with flapping buzzards, croaking hoarsely; possibly swearing in their own language on being interrupted at their morning meal.

It was not a cow, but a horse, which lay at the bottom of the ravine; a gray horse, partly eaten by buzzards, but with the brand still showing. Sleepy quickly noticed that its right foreleg was broken about half-way between knee and hock. Further investigation showed that the animal had been shot through the head, and that the shooter had held his gun so close that the powder had scorched the hair.

"Broke a leg and had to be shot," said Sleepy. "Not so very long ago."

They mounted and rode back to Marion, who had waited for them. Sleepy explained what caused the buzzards to congregate.

"What brand was on the animal?" she asked. Sleepy rubbed his nose thoughtfully. "Well, it happens to be a Double Bar 8."

"One of our horses?"

"Yeah—a gray. Weigh about a thousand. Got some dark spots on the rump, and its fetlocks are almost black."

"Why, that horse belonged to Buck! He didn't ride it often. But I never heard Buck say anything about shooting it."

"And pretty close to home, too," observed Jimmy.

The little ravine where the horse lay was not over an eighth of a mile from the Double Bar 8 stable.

"If the wind had blown down from that direction, we'd 'a' knowed it before this," grinned Sleepy.

The discovery of this horse interested Sleepy. He felt sure that Buck would have mentioned it at the ranch. The horse had either fallen into the ravine and broke a leg, or stepped into a hole. It was also very evident that the rider had mercifully put the animal out of its misery. And Sleepy wondered who, except some of the Taylor outfit, would be riding a Double Bar 8 horse so near the ranch.

He rode to Blue Wells that evening and met

Hashknife, whom he told about the dead horse. They found the sheriff at his office, and he let them in to see Buck Taylor. Buck was glad to see them, but denied knowing anything about the horse being dead.

" I ain't seen that horse for quite a while," he said. " He wasn't exactly a good cow-horse; so I let him drift. Plenty of speed, but he never seemed to *sabe* what it was all about. Who do yuh reckon killed him ? "

" Somebody must 'a' borrowed him, I s'pose," said Hashknife.

" Well, I wish we was out of here," sighed Buck. " With all this shootin' and dynamitin', I sure hate to stay here. I'd like to find the dirty snake that's doin' it all."

Hashknife and Sleepy left the jail and went to the livery-stable, where they had left Hashknife's horse that morning. Hashknife had nothing to say about his trip to Encinas, and Sleepy knew that questions were useless. Hashknife always worked on the theory that a secret is safe only with one person.

It was about ten o'clock when they approached the Double Bar 8, riding silently. There was a light in the ranch-house window, and as they drew closer they heard Jimmy's and Marion's voices blended in " After the Ball," accompanied by the old upright organ. The two cowboys drew rein and listened. Off to the left of them a horse nickered softly. They peered in that direction, thinking it was a loose horse.

Then they went on, their horses making little noise in the sandy road, and drew up just outside the patio entrance. They could hear Marion and Jimmy laughing, as Marion tried to strike the right chord on the old organ.

Something prompted Hashknife to walk from his horse to the patio entrance, where he stopped quickly. A man's voice snapped a warning, a streak of flame flashed toward him, and a bullet crashed into the corner of the entrance.

Two men were running toward the broken place in the wall, stumbling over the debris. Hashknife drew his six-shooter and fired twice, yelling at Sleepy to circle the wall. Another bullet whined off the adobe wall near him, as he started across the patio, heading for where the men had gone out.

Sleepy had dismounted, and he did not think to mount and ride. In fact, he hardly knew what it was all about. He ran around the wall and almost collided with Hashknife, who sprang out through where the dynamite had wrecked the wall.

" What the —— was it ? " panted Sleepy.

" Sh-h-h-h-h ! " whispered Hashknife. " Listen."

They stood against the ruined wall, straining their ears for the slightest sound. Then they heard the distant thud of running horses, growing fainter and fainter, as the riders faded away in the hills.

Hashknife swore softly, as he told Sleepy of the two men. Some one had extinguished the lamp in the ranch-house, and Sleepy called, telling them that everything was all right.

They found Marion and Jimmy on the back porch, and told them about the two men who had shot at Hashknife.

"Oh, I'm a fine guard!" said Jimmy bitterly. "Sleepy told me to keep an eye open. But we started singing, and——"

"Oh, it's all right," laughed Hashknife. "Nobody hurt. If we'd only gone over and investigated when that horse nickered, Sleepy, we'd 'a' had 'em cinched. But I didn't look for 'em to come back so soon. That's sure a puzzle. The further I go into this thing, the worse the fog gets.

"They wasn't over here by the house. They could 'a' looked in the window and seen who was in there. They might 'a' been waitin' for us to come back, but if they were, why did they let us walk in on 'em? I heard one of 'em snap a warnin'; so it kinda looks as though they didn't expect us just then."

"Do you think you hit either one of them?" asked Jimmy nervously.

Hashknife laughed.

"I was shootin' for general results. A man runnin' in the dark, jumpin' through a broken wall, is a hard target. And when yuh hit a man with a .45 in any spot, except his hands, arms, or the end of his nose, he won't go far; so I'll admit that I missed 'em."

For the next two nights Hashknife and Sleepy guarded the place, but no one came. The sheriff visited them, but they did not mention anything about the latest development. Hashknife was very thoughtful all the while, but admitted that he was getting nowhere in his deductions. He talked with Marion about Tex Alden and Le Moyne, and she seemed surprised when he told her that it was the general opinion that there was a rivalry over her between Tex and Le Moyne.

" Why, that is ridiculous," she told Hashknife. " Mr. Le Moyne used to drop in here once in a while, but he hasn't been here for over a month, except when they all came out to see the ruins of our bunk-house."

" As far as Tex is concerned, the opinion ain't far off, is it ? "

Marion flushed.

" I liked Tex all right," she admitted. " He is nice, as long as his temper doesn't run away with him. Tex has a bad temper, you know."

" And he hates Jimmy Legg, because Jimmy Legg happens to be here," observed Hashknife.

Marion looked at Hashknife, her eyes puzzled. Then—

" You don't think Tex was the one——" she hesitated.

" That tried to kill Jimmy ? " Hashknife finished for her.

" Oh, Tex couldn't do a thing like that, Hashknife ! "

" No ? " Hashknife smiled slowly. " Yuh don't think so ? "

Marion shook her head quickly.

" Not even if he was mad. He might be mad

enough for a moment to kill some one, but not to shoot from ambush."

" Well," grinned Hashknife, " I'll have to mark Tex Alden off my list of customers. It seems that Tex lost eight thousand dollars to Antelope Neal in a poker game. This was before we came here. Now I've been wonderin' how Tex could afford it."

" Yes, I heard about it, Hashknife. Tex works on a salary—the salary of a foreman—and he surely couldn't afford to lose that amount of money. In fact, I don't see where he got it."

" I know where he got it," smiled Hashknife. " But I don't see where he'll ever be able to pay it back."

Further than that Hashknife would not say, although Marion was curious to hear more about Tex Alden.

That evening Hashknife and Sleepy decided to visit Blue Wells, and talked things over with Jimmy.

" We may be back late," explained Hashknife. " There's a two-barrelled shotgun in the house, and I saw some shells on a shelf in the kitchen. You load that gun, Jimmy, and keep it handy. Lock all the doors, and be sure that every curtain is down. I don't look for any trouble, but yuh never can tell."

" I'll take care of everything," declared Jimmy. " And I'm not afraid. If anybody comes fooling around here to-night, I'll give them a surprise. I'll make it a point to keep awake."

They rode to Blue Wells after dark that night,

and found the three boys from the AK at the Oasis. Being Saturday night, there was quite a crowd in town, and the games were flourishing. Johnny Grant, Oyster Shell, and Eskimo Swensen welcomed Hashknife and Sleepy with open arms.

Tex Alden, Plenty Goode, and Ed Gast were in from the X Bar 6. Tex was cordial, and talked with Hashknife about the dynamiting. Hashknife knew that Tex was wondering where Jimmy Legg was, and finally Tex asked him if Marion wasn't afraid to stay at the ranch with only the Indian woman.

" Jimmy's out there," said Hashknife.

" Do yuh call that protection, Hartley ? "

Hashknife smiled, but said nothing. He was thinking of Jimmy and the short, ten-gauge Parker. Le Moyne and several of the men from the Santa Rita mine were in town. In the course of the evening Hashknife sat in on a poker game, in which Tex Alden, Plenty Goode, Johnny Grant, Scotty Olson, and Antelope Neal tried to outguess each other in the pastime. Sleepy and Oyster Shell quarrelled for hours over a bottle-pool game, which was being refereed by Eskimo Swensen, who had an injured hand, and was unable to play.

It was within an hour of daylight when Hashknife drew out of the poker game. He had won enough to make it worth his while, and Antelope Neal said he had never been more willing to cash in any man's chips and have his luck out of the game.

Sleepy was glad to go home.

" I've walked a hundred miles around that

darned pool table," he declared, as they left the Oasis. " A pile of blankets will look like a bank-roll to me."

There was a cold breeze blowing as they rode back to the Double Bar 8, and the crimson glow of the rising sun painted the crests of the eastern hills, as they rode in at the stable and put up their horses.

" Well, it don't look like any more dynamitin' had been done since we left," observed Sleepy, as they walked across the patio toward the rear door of the ranch-house.

" All is serene," said Hashknife, and as he spoke Nanah came to the doorway.

The Indian woman was a pitiful sight. Her face was streaked with blood, her dress torn, and she staggered wearily.

" For —— sake ! " gasped Hashknife. He took her by the shoulders. " What's wrong, Nanah ? What happened to you ? Where's Marion and Jimmy ? "

There was blood on her hair, and Hashknife could see that a livid welt ran from her right temple and disappeared in her mop of dishevelled black hair.

" I do' know," she choked. " Men come." She brushed her hand across her eyes, as though to clear her vision. " Have rag on faces. Knock Jimmy down. Take Marion, go that way." She leaned one shoulder heavily on Hashknife and pointed east.

" Yuh mean that masked men came and took Marion ? "

She nodded dumbly. Hashknife led her to a chair and made her sit down. The room showed signs of a struggle, and there were a number of blood stains on the floor and walls.

"What does it mean, Hashknife?" queried Sleepy anxiously.

"Where's Jimmy?" asked Hashknife.

Nanah shook her head. She didn't know where he was.

"I hear much noise," she said dumbly. "I come. Jimmy on floor. I run to door. Man hit me." Her hand went to her head. "I fall on floor. I do' know. I look from window, I see."

"You saw 'em goin' that way?"

"Yes."

"How many men, Nanah?"

"I do' know. I can't see very good. Too much blood."

"How long ago, Nanah?"

"I do' know. Pretty sick in head."

"She's got an awful wallop," said Sleepy. "Prob'ly got to the window, saw 'em pullin' out, and collapsed. What's the programme?"

Hashknife ran through the house and came back.

"The shotgun is gone," he said. "They've taken Marion toward Broken Cañon, but the devil only knows just where. Nanah, are you all right? We've got to get help. You stay here."

"Pretty good," she said. "You go quick."

They ran back to the stable and saddled their horses. The horses seemed to sense the need of speed, and the two boys mounted on the run.

Sleepy stood in his stirrups, his lips opened in a soundless yell. This was action. They swung around the point of a hill, heading up through a swale, a mile or more from the ranch-house. Hashknife spurred in close to Sleepy.

"Get the sheriff and all the boys yuh can get together, and head for Broken Cañon, Sleepy. I'm goin' back."

Sleepy did not question him. He had spent too many years with Hashknife to question any action of the tall cowboy. He merely nodded, drew his hat down over his brow and headed for Blue Wells to gather a posse, while Hashknife drew rein, turned around, and went back.

The poker game had just broken up, when Sleepy dropped off his horse at the door of the Oasis, and panted out his story.

"Good ——— !" exclaimed Tex Alden. "There's more than one hole-in-the-ground in Broken Cañon ! Let's go ! "

Scotty Olson, the sheriff, got his horse, and they rode out of Blue Wells, nine strong ; Olson, Sleepy, Tex, Gast, Goode, Johnny Grant, Eskimo, and Oyster Shell. There was nothing for them to work on, except that Nanah had said that the men had gone toward Broken Cañon.

CHAPTER XIII

CAPTURED

IT would have been difficult for any of Jimmy's friends to have recognised him, unless they examined him closely. His face was plastered with gore, one eye swelled shut and his lip cut. He had no hat, one sleeve of his shirt flapped behind him, like a streamer tied to his shoulder. He had no saddle. In the crook of one elbow he carried the heavy, double-barrel shotgun. That was the extent of his armament. It was the first time he had ever ridden a bareback horse, and he was having plenty of difficulty in staying on the animal's back.

Jimmy was still in a daze—but a very determined sort of a daze. All night long he had stayed awake, guarding the ranch-house. Dawn was in sight when he dozed, only to be awakened by a knock on the back door.

"Is that you, Hashknife?" he had asked, and it seemed to him that an affirmative reply had been given. At any rate he had opened the door, only to find himself confronted by three masked men. And before he had time to move, one of the men struck him across the head with a gun barrel, knocking him down. But the blow was a glancing one, and did not knock him out.

Badly dazed, he got to his feet, trying to fight, and one of the men drove several smashing blows to his head and face, knocking him out. He had little idea of what happened after that, until returning consciousness gave him a blurred vision of these men taking Marion out of the house. He had tried to get up, but his limbs refused to function.

He saw Nanah crawl to a window, where she managed to look out, before she crumpled to the floor. It seemed years to him before he could get to the window, but his vision had cleared sufficiently to enable him to see the riders going away.

Summoning up every bit of his courage, he secured the shotgun, and managed to stagger to the stable, where he bridled a horse, crawled on its back, and followed them. He was like a man riding through a fog. He had no idea of direction. With his right hand he tried to wipe the blood out of his eyes, but gave it up.

He remembered that there were three men. But that did not matter. He had two cartridges in that shotgun, and he could use the gun as a club, after those shots were gone, he decided. He was no longer the smiling James Eaton Legg, but Jimmy Legg—cowboy. The book-keeper was gone entirely, and in his place was a bloody-faced young man, who wanted to kill somebody with a shotgun.

Jimmy did not know how long he had ridden. The sun was shining, and his head ached badly. He wanted to stop and lie down, but he kept on going, laughing grimly to himself. The horse stopped, and Jimmy realised that it was standing

on the edge of a cañon. He did not know that
this was Broken Cañon. Names meant nothing
to him. The horse turned to the right and followed
the cañon rim. At times they swung far to the
right, passing around the head of tributary cañons,
but always coming back to the main cañon
rim.

Jimmy's reason was coming back to him now,
but it only made the incidents more vivid in his
mind. He realised that he had left his six-shooter
at the ranch, and that the two cartridges in his gun
were all he had.

The horse picked its way among a piled-up mass
of big rocks and tangled brush, and came out on
sort of mesa. The cañon widened here, its depths
purple and gold in the rising sun. On the far side
of the cañon were sandstone minarets, gleaming
gold-like at the top, banded with red, fading into
a deep purple below the sun-line.

But Jimmy had no eyes for the beauties of the
sunrise. He could see several people near the
cañon rim, a quarter of a mile away, their horses
etched in relief against the gray of a huge upthrust
slap of gray stone. Then he saw two of the riders
turn and ride directly away from the cañon, going
at a swift gallop.

He saw the others ride out of sight, as if going
down into the cañon. Jimmy felt sure that the
first two were men, and if Marion was one of the
party, she must have been one of those to go into
the cañon. He spurred his horse down through the
tangle of brush, heading for that huge gray slab,

regardless of mesquite, cactus, and other thorny things that tore at his legs.

He reached the spot, and found that a trail led down into the cañon, partly masked by the granite cliff. He could see where it disappeared around a sharp corner, and he wondered how any one could ride down there without being scraped off. But he knew there was only one thing to do—and that was to head down the trail. Clutching the mane of the horse in one hand, and holding his precious shotgun close to his body, he spurred the horse down the narrow trail, leaning away from the cañon depth, but letting the horse take its own gait.

Jimmy had little time to do any observation work. In fact, he had almost forgotten that he was following any one, as his mind was wholly taken up in fear of this rough trail. Suddenly he realised that he was almost at the bottom. He could see the piled-up boulders in the bottom, the glint of a small stream.

His horse slipped, and its pawing hoofs sent a shower of stones off the trail, crashing down through the dry foliage, rattling off the rocks at the bottom. Jimmy had slipped to its rump, but managed to claw his way back. He had dropped his reins, but was not making any effort to recover them for fear of frightening the horse.

Suddenly he felt a tug at his leg, and the horse seemed to fairly fall from under him, while the crash of a shot echoed back and forth from the sides of the cañon. Jimmy sprawled above the horse, falling across his shotgun. For several moments he did not move. Then he drew up his left leg. The bullet had scored him slightly just above the knee-cap, doing little damage.

He tried to crawl away, but the bank was too steep. He turned over on his back, twisting sideways, trying to see below him, but could see nobody. Ignorantly inviting another shot, he crawled to his feet and stepped down past the horse, which was so badly hurt that it scarcely moved. Another shot crashed out, the bullet passing so close to Jimmy that he wasn't sure it did not hit him. Instinctively jerking aside, his feet flew from under him, and he cascaded down to the bottom of the cañon, taking a conglomeration of brush and rocks with him, which slowed up his progress enough to enable him to reach the bottom, uninjured, except for numerous cuts and bruises and the sacrifice of a goodly portion of his raiment.

But he clung to his shotgun. Nothing short of general cataclysm would make Jimmy Legg let loose of that gun. It was his one hope. He landed in a clump of huge boulders, while over him poured more gravel and rubbish, which had followed in his wake.

In fact, he was so covered with debris that the masked man, holding a ready rifle, who came looking for a dead man, did not see him for a few moments. This man stepped cautiously up on a ledge of rock, about a hundred feet from the sand and brush that covered Jimmy, who lifted the shotgun, pointed it in his general direction, and pulled the trigger.

The big shotgun roared like a cannon, kicked

Jimmy so hard that it fairly dusted him off. He got to his feet, panting the breath back into his tortured lungs, as he surged forward, looking for concealment. The man dropped off the rock with a yelp of amazement, possibly tinged with injury. A dozen buckshot are not to be faced lightly.

Jimmy landed behind a boulder, rubbed his shoulder, which was numb from the recoil of the shotgun, and began crawling ahead. He peered over a boulder, and a bullet filled his eyes with rock-dust.

" I guess I didn't kill him," observed Jimmy, and angled his way to another boulder. He had only one shot left now. Another boulder seemed to beckon him, and a bullet struck just short of him, cutting his right cheek with flying gravel. Jimmy curled up behind the boulder and took stock of himself.

" This won't do," he decided. " I'm doing all the moving. If I could only get to that boulder, I could crawl up the other side and be on a level with him."

It was a long chance, but Jimmy took it, and he sprawled in behind the cover of brush and rocks, while a ricocheting bullet hummed away up the cañon, like an angry bee. The heavy screen of brush enabled him to crawl up out of the water-course, and it seemed that this was just what the other man did not want, because he sent bullet after bullet through the brush, picking spots at intervals of a few feet.

But in spite of his bombardment, Jimmy reached

the top of the washout, where he sprawled on his face, panting heavily. The man put a few more bullets through the brush, which proved to Jimmy that the shooter did not know that he had reached the top.

Jimmy's face was bleeding badly, and his mouth was salty from sweat and gore. He found that his leg wound was also bleeding considerably, but gave him little pain. He took time to wrap his handkerchief around it to keep out the dirt.

Then he began crawling again, snaking his way through the brush, trying to see the man who wanted to kill him. He came to the fringe of the brush, and peered out. He could see the man now ; that is, he could see his head and shoulders and rifle. He was still watching the place where Jimmy had dropped behind the boulder, before climbing out of the washout.

Farther down the cañon he could see the two horses, and on one was the figure of a girl, evidently roped tightly, because she was having difficulty in looking back toward the scene of conflict.

Jimmy studied the man, and tried to map out a plan of attack. He was about a hundred feet away, but Jimmy thought the target too small to take a chance on his remaining shot. He saw the man look back toward the horses. He was evidently getting impatient. Brush grew fairly heavy along the slope, and Jimmy pondered the chances he might have to work his way to the horses without being seen. It would be a dangerous move, he decided. Anyway, he liked the cover of the boulder-strewn brush, and as long as the man was willing to wait, he would, too.

He saw the man take off his hat and lift it above the top of the rock. It rather puzzled Jimmy. He jerked it down quickly. Then he exposed it in another place. It suddenly struck Jimmy that this man was trying to draw his fire, and his blood-caked features cracked into a grin.

An insane desire to yell at this man gripped at him. He wanted to laugh, to joke this man. But his better judgment bade him be still. He saw the man move forward to another boulder, where he repeated the cap-lifting. Jimmy realised that this man was getting impatient to have the fight finished.

The man kept moving ahead, until he was masked from Jimmy, who crawled out of the brush and headed for the rim of the washout again, trading sides with the other man. For about thirty feet Jimmy crawled swiftly, dropped behind some cover, and waited.

It was about five minutes later that he saw the man again. He had moved farther up the cañon, possibly thinking that Jimmy had made his escape. By standing up, Jimmy could get a good look at this man, who was too far away for Jimmy to take a chance with the shotgun ; so Jimmy dropped back into the washout, bent down low, and headed in the general direction of the horses.

But he had not escaped detection. A bullet sang past his ear, and he stumbled over a boulder, falling sidewise into a cut on the left-hand side of the washout. To the shooter, it possibly appeared as if he had been struck. Jimmy was half-standing, half-lying in the cut, when he heard the drumming of footsteps, as the man hurried forward. There was no chance of concealment there.

It seemed as if the man were almost over him when he raised up, shoving the shotgun barrel over the rim of the washout. The man jerked to a stop, only fifty feet away, firing his rifle from his hip, just as Jimmy pressed the trigger. The bullet struck just in front of Jimmy's face, filling his nose, eyes, and mouth with dirt, and the kick of the shotgun sent him running backward down the short slope, where he hooked his heel on a rock, and sprawled on his back.

It was several moments before he could get up. He felt weak, nauseated, as he spat out the dirt, blinked tearfully, and climbed to the top of the washout. Out there on the flat ground was the man, sprawling on his face, his rifle flung aside.

Jimmy did not go near him. He sighed heavily and headed for the horses, where Marion's white face and astonished eyes drove every other thought from his mind. Neither of them spoke as he cut the ropes which bound her, and she got stiffly from the saddle, clinging to him.

" You—you came, didn't you, Jimmy? " she whispered hoarsely.

" Yea-a-ah, I sure did." Jimmy grinned on one side of his face, because the other was glued tightly with gore. " It was quite a trip. This has been a tough season, Marion."

It was rather inane conversation, but under the circumstances it was excusable.

The man was trying to sit up, and Marion pointed to him breathlessly. Jimmy went staggering out to him, a loose-jointed young man, who had been hurt so many times that he was numb all over. He picked up the rifle and stepped back, tottering on his feet.

"You better stay where you are," he told the masked man. "You ain't so awful tough."

Jimmy had heard Johnny Grant use that expression, and it seemed to fit the occasion. He turned his head and called to Marion.

"Can you lead the horses up here, Marion? We've got to pack this lead-filled person to a doctor, or he won't live to be hung."

CHAPTER XIV

WHO GOT THE PAY-ROLL ?

WHEN Hashknife turned back to the Double Bar 8
it was because of a single theory. He was fairly
positive that Marion had not been kidnapped by
those men because they wanted her ; but that they
had had reasons of more importance to them than
the mere capture of a young lady. Hashknife
wasn't sure just what this was, but he had a
suspicion—at least, enough suspicion to send him
back to the ranch, instead of heading a posse over
to the breaks of Broken Cañon.

He rode his horse into the stable, unsaddled
quickly, turned it into the corral, and ran to the
house, where he found Nanah bathing her head in
a basin of water. He explained to her the necessity
of locking the house, covering the windows, and of
keeping out of sight.

Without question she obeyed him, and he went
back to the stable, climbed to the little loft, and
sprawled near the window, concealed by a screen
of hay. He could not see over the ranch-house,
except at a distance, but his little window gave
him a fairly good view of the country toward Broken
Cañon.

Apollo wandered about the patio, possibly wondering why no one was about. Mocking-birds sang from the twisted vines along the walls, and little lizards scuttled here and there over the debris of the former bunk-house. Hashknife yawned and waited, wondering what success Sleepy had had in gathering a posse.

He had been there over an hour when his keen eyes detected two riders, who seemed to be coming swiftly toward the ranch from the north-east. Blue Wells was almost directly north. He wondered if some of the posse had turned back from going to Broken Cañon and were coming to the ranch.

When about a mile from the ranch they swung due west, passing from Hashknife's vision. He went to the rear of the loft, and peered from a crack. The riders came into sight, swinging in toward the ranch again, but disappeared into the cañon where Hashknife had captured Plenty Goode, following the mysterious shot from the hill.

It took them several minutes to cross the cañon, and he saw them draw rein in the heavy cover, where they stayed for about five minutes, evidently studying the ranch buildings. Their elevation gave them a good view of the whole country.

Finally they rode down toward the stable. Hashknife was unable to recognise them, nor did he recognise their horses—a roan and a gray. Softly Hashknife went back to his former position at the window. He heard the riders come in behind the stable, where they stopped. After a few moments he heard them in the stable, talking softly. One of them laughed, but their conversation was too indistinct for Hashknife to hear what was said.

He was so intent on listening that he was not aware they were out of the stable until he turned his head and saw them going into the patio.

It rather amused Hashknife to see that these men were both masked. One of them went to the ranch-house door, finding it locked. It was evident to Hashknife that these men were sure that every one had left the ranch. They conferred together for a moment, and one of them came toward Hashknife, stopping on the ruins of the bunk-house, while the other man swung up on the wall near the corner of the ranch-house and scanned the country.

Slowly Hashknife slid back across the floor, until he reached the ladder, which led down from the loft. He went down the ladder and walked softly to the door, where he peered around the edge. He could hear the sound of some one digging ; the dull thud of adobe bricks being thrown aside, but he could not see either of the men now.

Drawing his six-shooter, Hashknife went slowly and carefully across the space between the stable door and the patio wall. He could hear the digging plainly now. Then he heard one of the men snap out a curse. It was evidently the man on the wall, because the answering voice was just beyond.

" What's the matter ? "

" That posse must 'a' seen us ! They're comin' ! "

The two men were running now, and Hashknife expected them to come through the broken wall past him, but instead they went out the south entrance of the patio, possibly with the intention of keeping the ranch buildings between them and the approaching posse, and circling back to their horses.

Disregarding the fact that the odds were two to one, Hashknife ran swiftly along the wall, coming out within fifty feet of the two men, who were humped over, running as low as possible. There was no time for them to turn; nothing to do but fight or surrender. It was still a hundred feet to the cover of the brush, and Hashknife was between them and the stable. But neither of them thought of surrender. Hashknife fired, as the two men whirled to a stop and drew their guns. One of them went to his knees, and his bullet tore up a spurt of dust half-way between him and Hashknife, and the other man's bullet sang wide of its target. He fired again, but his bullet went skyward, because the shock of Hashknife's next bullet threw him backward. The man who was on his knees fired again, but so wildly that Hashknife did not even hear the bullet.

Then he tried to get to his feet, pitched forward on his face, and lay still. The other man did not move, except that he half turned over. Hashknife went slowly up to them, his jaw shut grimly. He had shot deliberately, slowly—only twice. Even with the two-to-one odds, the advantage had been with him, because he had been ready for the battle.

Hashknife did not make any examination of the

men. He heard the drumming of hoofs, as the posse rode up, and in a few moments they were surrounded by excited men—the nine men who had ridden out of Blue Wells with Sleepy.

" My ——, it's Al Porter and Chet Le Moyne ! " exclaimed the sheriff, tearing the masks off the two men. " Hartley, what does this mean ? "

He came to Hashknife, gripping his arm.

" It means that an officer of the law went wrong," said Hashknife coldly.

" But how ? " demanded the excited sheriff. " This needs more explanation than that, Hartley."

" Go easy," advised Sleepy, who turned to Hashknife. " We wasn't quite to the Broken Cañon, when we spotted these two riders. They were headin' this way, foggin' to beat —— ; so we follered."

" Good thing yuh did, Sleepy."

Questions volleyed at Hashknife, while others examined Le Moyne and Porter, but Hashknife brushed them all aside.

" They're both as dead as herrin'," said Johnny Grant.

Two more riders came—Antelope Neal and Lee Barnhardt.

" We missed the posse ; so came here to see what we could do to help," said Neal.

Barnhardt squinted at the dead men, but said nothing.

" Will yuh please tell us what it means ? " asked the sheriff. " You ain't told anythin' yet, yuh know, Hartley."

Hashknife smiled grimly.

" There ain't much to tell, Scotty. These men came here, wearin' masks. They tried to get away when they saw yuh comin', but I blocked 'em, and we shot it out."

" Oh, I can see that ! But——"

" Good —— ! Here comes some more ! " Johnny Grant's yell turned all interest away from Hashknife.

It was Marion and Jimmy on one horse, leading another horse, on which was roped a swaying figure of a man, his body slouched forward until his face was almost buried in his chest. Jimmy was riding behind Marion, clinging to her, while he swayed weakly, a silly smile on his dirty face.

Men ran to them, while others unroped the sagging figure on the other horse. It was Dug Haley, of the Santa Rita mine. He was conscious, but unable to stand. Willing hands lifted Jimmy off the horse, but his left leg was too sore for him to stand on it for several moments.

" I—I got him," Jimmy told Hashknife hoarsely. " Filled him full of shot. We had a regular battle down in the cañon."

The sheriff was goggling from one to another, trying to get things straightened out to his own mind. Hashknife went to Marion.

" Tell us what you know about it, Marion," he said.

" Oh, I don't know very much, Hashknife. Three masked men came, and they—I heard the noise, when they fought with Jimmy, and came out to

see what it was about. They had knocked him
down, and I thought he was dead.

"They told me not to be afraid, and that everything would be all right. It seems that I wasn't to
be hurt. They put me on a horse, and we went
to Broken Cañon, where two of the men turned
back. They were masked all the time ; so I wasn't
just sure who they were, because they changed their
voices.

"One man took me down into the cañon, and I
think he heard Jimmy coming. Anyway, he tied
the horses and went back toward the bottom of the
trail. I heard a lot of shooting, and I was sure
somebody was trying to help me, but I never
thought it was Jimmy, until he shot Dug Haley.

"We had a hard time getting him on a horse,
because Jimmy was so weak he couldn't help much.
But we made it. We've got to get Jimmy to a
doctor, because he's all cut to pieces."

Haley was sitting on the ground, goggling at
every one. He had lost a lot of blood, but his
mind was clear. Hashknife saw him eyeing the
bodies of Le Moyne and Porter ; so he stepped
over to him.

"Haley," he said kindly, "the game is up.
You better come clean, because yo're the last of the
three men who stole that pay-roll. Al Porter did
not go to Encinas the night of the robbery, and
more than that, he and that girl of his busted up
two months ago. Which one of yuh rode Buck
Taylor's gray horse that night, and had to kill it
up there in that little cañon ? "

"That was me." Haley spoke hoarsely. "Oh, I might as well admit it. Le Moyne schemed it, and we helped him. But our luck broke bad. Le Moyne had to be at the depot when the train came in, and Porter had to be on the other side of Broken Cañon to pick up a freight early in the mornin'—or when one come along ; so it was up to me to take the money to Santa Rita, where we was goin' to hide it.

" I kinda got off in my bearin's, in the dark, and found myself too far south. Then that gray horse fell and busted a leg. , I had to kill it, yuh see. Then I had all that gold to carry. It wasn't safe to cache it in the hills, because I didn't know the country well enough."

Haley smiled grimly.

" I seen the light from the ranch-house, and I was sure it was the Double Bar 8 ; so I packed the gold down here, lookin' for a place to hide it. Back of the bunk-house I found a hole under the foundation. I scratched a match and looked it over. It wasn't big enough for anythin' but a small dog to get through ; so I shoved that money under the bunk-house, and went back to the mine."

" And then dynamited the bunk-house, eh ? " queried the sheriff.

" Like ——, we did ! That's why we kidnapped the girl. We wanted to draw everybody away, so we could dig the money out of the ruins. But we wasn't goin' to hurt her. I was to keep her in the cañon until about noon, and then let her come home. Our idea was to get Hartley and Stevens away from here long enough to let us get the money."

" And it's still under all that adobe, eh ? " smiled Hashknife.

" If Le Moyne and Porter didn't get it out. I wish you'd get me to a doctor. I'm full of buckshot. That —— tenderfoot ! We didn't count him in a-tall."

" I didn't need to be counted," croaked Jimmy. " But what I want to know is, who shot me, and who blew up the bunk-house ? "

Hashknife stepped over and put a hand on Barnhardt's shoulder. The Blue Wells attorney's lips went white, and he tried to draw away.

" You tell 'em about it," advised Hashknife. " Just be a man and speak yore little piece, Barnhardt."

" Me ? " whispered Barnhardt. " Why—why— I don't know——"

" Do yuh want me to tell it ? "

Barnhardt's legs jiggled nervously and he wet his lips with his tongue, while his Adam's apple jiggled convulsively.

" There's nun-nothing to—to——"

" Then I'll tell it," said Hashknife. " And if Mr. Barnhardt don't stand still, keep his hands where they are and not try to scratch his ribs around the spot where his gun hangs in a shoulder-holster, I'll betcha somebody will add him to the list of casualties.

" Mr. Barnhardt is a cousin of Mrs. Martha Eaton, of Chicago, who owns this ranch. For several years Mr. Barnhardt has handled all the affairs of the X Bar 6. In fact he grew rich, handling her stock interests. But she was a simple old lady, with quite extensive holdings, and she had faith in Mr. Barnhardt.

" Now, if I make any mistakes, I hope Mr. Barnhardt won't interrupt, until I'm finished. A short time ago Mrs. Eaton became an invalid, and was unable to handle her own business. I reckon the doctors have told her that she won't live more than one year more.

" Still bein' of sound mind, she decided to make out a will, and in this will she goes kinda hay-wire, like old folks do sometimes ; so she picks out a young feller, whose name was James Eaton Legg, a son of her sister, and wills him the X Bar 6, with the provision that within a year he be able to present proof that he is capable of runnin' this here ranch.

" And about that time she turns her affairs over to Leesom and Brand, a law firm in Chicago, who, after lookin' things over, decides that the returns from the X Bar 6 need investigatin'. It kinda looks to them as though that ranch ought to pay more dividends. Accordin' to their reports, there's too many cows out here, and not enough revenue.

" They takes it up with the Cattle Association of this here State, the same of which sends me and Sleepy up here to work on the round-up and send in a tally of the X Bar 6. It appears that Jimmy Legg accidentally drifts in here, tryin' make a

cowpuncher out of himself; and our friend Barnhardt, knowin' that Jimmy might beat him out of
a lot of money, decides to put him out of
commission.

"And I'm not sure, but I think Mr. Barnhardt
stole one of my letters from the Chicago lawyers,
and found out what we was doin' here; so he
plants dynamite under the bunk-house, after he
misses two well-meant shots. Oh, he was a friendly
sort of a jigger. Now, Barnhardt, tell us yore
story."

But the Blue Wells attorney merely goggled,
trying to deny it all with a shake of his head.

"You planned to make a getaway, yuh know,"
smiled Hashknife. "Yore little vacation was goin'
to be permanent, but I cracked yore safe the night
before, because I knew yuh wouldn't go away
broke, and I wanted time to land the train robbers.
Yeah, I've got all yore stuff. It'll send yuh over
for a long time."

"This is funny," said Tex Alden. "I had a
letter from that same firm, askin' me a few questions. It kinda looked to me as though Barnhardt
was playin' crooked; so I held out that eight
thousand and faked a loss to Antelope Neal, who
was in on the game with me. I wanted to see if
Barnhardt was crooked enough to doctor the books
for me, but he was pretty shrewd, and I really
got afraid he might have me arrested for embezzlement and put me in pretty bad; so me and Neal
marked all those bills and I gave 'em back to him."

Hashknife held out his hand to Tex.

" I couldn't figure yuh out for quite a while," said Hashknife, smiling.

" Barnhardt sure tried to put me in bad, Hartley. He told me about that pay-roll comin' in, because he thought I'd do anythin' to pay him back that eight thousand, and he also wanted his split of the thirty thousand dollars."

Jimmy had gone to the house, and now he came staggering back, followed by Geronimo, barking joyfully. The sheriff turned from handcuffing Barnhardt, and stared at the dog.

" We had him in the cellar," laughed Hashknife. " He's the dog that was on the express car, and Jimmy Legg is the big burly who fought with the messenger."

The boys crowded around Jimmy, slapping him on the back ; which, under the circumstances, did not appeal to Jimmy, who was just beginning to find out how sore he really was.

" Lemme alone, you man-chasers ! " he yelped. " I was tough for an hour or so, but I'm sure tender now."

" Talks like a cowpuncher," said Eskimo gravely.

" Looks like a cowpuncher," added Johnny.

" Fights like one," groaned Dug Haley. " When yuh get through throwin' bouquets, I wish you'd take me to a doctor."

Hashknife grinned at the wreck of what had been James Eaton Legg, the book-keeper, and nodded solemnly.

" I reckon we'll be able to tell Leesom and Brand that Jimmy Legg has qualified," he said earnestly.

" And if I was Jimmy Legg, I'd put on some clothes," said Sleepy. " Cowboy, yo're a fright."

Jimmy grinned, started toward the house, followed by Marion. But Jimmy shoved her ahead of him, because he just remembered that he had slid half-way down Broken Cañon, sitting down. Tex looked after them, a half-smile on his face, as he turned to Hashknife.

The posse was putting the bodies in the ranch wagon, and two of the men were assisting the sheriff, who had put Dug Haley on the wagon-seat, and was helping the dazed lawyer to mount his sway-backed horse. The handcuffs bothered Barnhardt, and he was breathing like an asthmatic.

" You don't act very sore about it," said Hash-knife, nodding toward where Marion and Jimmy were disappearing into the house.

Tex shrugged his shoulders.

" I know when I'm whipped," he said, with just a trace of bitterness in his voice. " It seems that Legg didn't. If yuh want me to sign that affidavit, regardin' his ability, bring it around. Leesom and Brand know I wouldn't be fool enough to wish him on to me as a boss, unless he was capable—and I'll teach him all I know."

" That's square enough," nodded Hashknife. " Wait until I saddle my bronc, and I'll ride to Blue Wells with yuh. Me and Sleepy have got to peddle a couple of horses before that train pulls through."

" Yo're not leavin' so soon, are yuh ? "

Marion and Jimmy were coming from the ranch

house, and with them was Nanah, her head bandaged up. Geronimo circled them, barking with joy. Jimmy was clad in a baggy pair of overalls and a shirt three sizes too large for him. The face-washing operation had opened the cuts on Jimmy's face, and he was beginning to look like a warpath Indian.

" We'll all three ride in the buggy," said Marion. " Jimmy is too weak and sore to ride a horse, and Nanah won't."

Tex offered to hitch up the horse, and Marion went with him to the stable. Hashknife drew Jimmy aside.

" I reckon you've made good, Jimmy," Hashknife said slowly. " I'll see that the right report goes to Leesom and Brand. You'll marry and settle down on the X Bar 6, I reckon, eh ? "

" Marry and settle down ? "

" Yea—sure. You'll marry her, won't yuh ? "

" Marion ? Why——"

Jimmy hesitated, his eyes turning toward the stable door, where Marion and Tex were standing. Marion was looking down at the ground, but now she looked up at him, a smile on her face. Tex started to reach toward her, realised that he had an audience, and they both stepped inside the stable. Jimmy grinned and shook his head.

" Why, no, I don't reckon I will, Hashknife. That whips me."

And Jimmy wondered why Hashknife laughed so suddenly and walked to his horse. He did not know that Tex had admitted defeat, too. When the buggy, with its three occupants started up the road toward Blue Wells, with Tex Alden riding beside it, far in the distance they could see a lone rider—Hashknife Hartley, riding swiftly to join Sleepy, that they might dispose of their horses and catch the first train out of town. Their work was done—and the other side of the hill was calling.

TO THE READER

If you enjoyed this book, you will be glad to know that there are many others just as well written, just as interesting, to be had in the Fiction House Press Library.

You will find the Fiction House Press Library online at

www.FictionHousePress.com

www.ingramcontent.com/pod-product-compliance
Lightning Source LLC
Chambersburg PA
CBHW070519030726
47503CB00004B/1315